Volume Six

AIRSHIP 27 PRODUCTIONS

Sinbad-The New Voyages Volume Six

"Sinbad in the Land of Fire & Ice" ©2019 Nancy Hansen
"Mages of the Obsidian Shard" © 2019 Greg Hatcher

Published by Airship 27 Productions
www.airship27.com
www.airship27hangar.com

Interior illustrations © 2019 Jesus Rodriguez & Rob Davis
Cover illustration © 2019 Adam Shaw

Editor: Ron Fortier
Associate Editor: Gordon Dymowski
Promotions Manager: Michael Vance
Production and design by Rob Davis.

ISBN: 978-1-946183-70-5

Printed in the United States of America

10 9 8 7 6 5 4 3 2 1

Sinbad
the New Voyages Volume 6

TABLE of CONTENTS

SINBAD IN THE LAND OF FIRE AND ICE

by
Nancy A. Hansen

"Sinbad, Allah be praised, I am so glad to see you!" exclaimed Omar.

The short and stocky man was sweating profusely and puffing for breath, as he was forced to trot in order to match the long-legged stride of his tall and limber captain. As they skirted the seawall on their way down to the docks, he marveled at the pace Sinbad set so early in the morning. You'd never know this sepia-hued son of a Moorish princess and a Nubian Prince had been out drinking and carousing for twenty one days, for he showed little sign of such indulgences. To revel in excess was ever Sinbad's habit if he was stuck in port for any length of time, and they had been in Debal far longer than the captain of the Blue Nymph had wished while his ship was being refitted and her brand new navigational devices were installed by skilled craftsmen. Sinbad El Ari was a restless man by nature, and even more so when away from the sea. He took to the types of illicit amusements that wealthy, handsome men find enjoyable—gambling, drinking, and sampling the charms of numerous beautiful women—without ever becoming dissolute or corrupt in any way.

"Omar, I didn't think you cared so much," Sinbad joked, actually jovial in spite of the nagging headache from too much expensive wine and lovemaking the night past. Other than his eyes being a bit bloodshot, you'd never know how much he'd imbibed, or how hard General Dahir's trio of nubile and quite amorous daughters had labored to wear him out. It had been an enchanting end to a forced vacation, but now he was ready to go to sea again, providing the Blue Nymph was prepared to sail.

"What of my ship?" Sinbad asked the blustering little man with a smile as he spotted her down the quay. The indigo sail was still furled, but she was in the water at last, and the workmen were putting the finishing touches on the figurehead, where his navigation devices were being installed.

"That is exactly what I need to talk to you about!" Omar said more than a bit irritably. He stopped to catch his breath, gasping and holding

his sides. "You see, we have had some issue with the placement of those...
fabricated crystals, or whatever they are supposed to be."

"They belong in her eyes, of course," Sinbad answered simply, and
for a moment he peered quizzically at the still wheezing and red-faced
man beside him. Omar was his crew master and the most loyal first mate
Sinbad had ever hired. A perpetual complainer and nagger, he also never
honey-coated the truth, which made him reliable. "Is something wrong?"

"Perhaps you will think so," Omar said darkly as he trod ahead and led
the way down to the ship, where already Sinbad's able companions Tishimi,
Ralf, and even the perpetually absent Gaul archer Henri Delacrois had
gathered to watch the final preparations, which were to be done under
guard. "I am told we must reconsider where we install these devices. You
will see, once you truly look at her," he added with distaste.

"Now you have my curiosity piqued," Sinbad said lightly, though his
quick mind was already churning moodily over yet another delay. He
wanted to catch the tide and be gone this very day!

"Sinbad, come look at this," Henri called, his sharp eyes having spotted
his captain. He shouldered his bow and beckoned urgently. "I have told
them they cannot place the crystals there, but they don't listen to me."

"No one in his right mind ever listens to you," Ralf commented with
a smirk half hidden by his bristling beard. The tall, blonde giant of a
Norseman was leaning on his axe head with arms folded, his feet planted
wide around the knob end of the haft.

A lightly built but deceptively powerful and accomplished samurai,
Tishimi Osara remained silent with her face impassive, but her rigid
stance and the way she stroked her twin blades told everyone she was
displeased with something. Her head was tilted back with shining ebony
locks streaming down over her black silk clad shoulders as green eyes
watched the workmen well above with circumspect interest.

The issue did become apparent once Sinbad came up closer to the bow.
Sinbad's ship the Blue Nymph was named for her colorful figurehead of
a mermaid, with her lower half a silvered fish, and from the waist up, a
very lovely and buxom naked woman, her long arms thrust out behind
her embracing the bow, and flowing hair streaming backward as if wind
tossed. To be effective, the twin devices Sinbad had ordered made of
various metals and crystals within a copper spiral, each captured in a cone
shaped pyramid of the clearest resin available, must be at the very apex of
that figurehead in order to guide the ship. Sinbad had assumed that they
would be installed in the mermaid's eyes, but her eyes were not her most

prominent and forward thrusting features.

"Oh ho, I see what you mean now!" he said with a grin as he stroked his pointed beard and watched the second of the very expensive and highly controversial etheric navigation devices being fitted into a channel that had been drilled into her rather ample left breast. "Well, it's not what I had in mind, but it should still work."

"I don't understand! How can she see through her teats–" Omar began, but Sinbad cut him off.

"They don't actually work that way; they just need to be as far forward as we can manage so they have a clear sweep of the sea before us. In all honesty, I'm not really sure how they actually accomplish whatever it is they do," he admitted with uncharacteristic frankness. "Still, I am eager to try them out. Since this is nearly finished, we shall set sail today, so get the crew aboard and make sure we're properly supplied." He headed up the gangplank to speak with the carpenters, and double check that these things were going to remain in place no matter how rough the seas got.

Omar trotted after him. "Where are we going this time Sinbad?" he asked.

"I'm sure we'll soon find out," the taller man said eagerly as he headed forward to climb out on the bow and take a closer look at the handiwork of the best men money and influence could buy him.

While all ports had their delights, Sinbad soon tired of them. It was wonderful to be back at sea; to smell again the salt breeze untainted by more pungent land scents, to hear the flap of the sail overhead and the frothing of the water alongside, and feel the deck heaving beneath his feet. He initially set a general course out of the Arabian Sea and into the wider Indian Ocean. Once he was safely in the open, he would try out his new navigation devices.

The one thing that had not been clear in the instructions Sinbad had retrieved for concocting these extraordinary inventions was just exactly how to activate them. The phrase, *'any spirited air shall enlighten your way'* made no sense! It actually sounded rather mystical and just a bit sinister, but it would not do to let any of the crew learn that before necessary. He focused instead on whetting their appetite by reassuring them they'd be seeing lands previously unknown, and finding treasure beyond their wildest dreams, as he had heard about this from the elderly Sindhi sailor who first told him of the devices. Sinbad himself wondered, just what remarkable adventures would this bring?

No doubt there would be hazards as well. Danger was something he scoffed at, for he had lived through so many things that would have felled lesser men that he actually welcomed a bit of precariousness to any journey. It was like the addition of spice to roasting meat—without it life would be banal and bland indeed. A trip seasoned by just the right amount of peril was something to be looked forward to. Afterward a man truly knew himself to be alive, and he had stories to tell that would bring others flocking to his side to listen and toast his success. Ah, this was adventure at its finest!

Sinbad had purposely chosen that first day for them to leave because the night would feature no moon, and the outgoing tide would be at its strongest. If these devices were going to provide some sort of guiding beam, they would be able to see it best on a dark night away from harbor lanterns. The twin cones of composite materials had proved quite expensive to procure and manufacture, and so they were rather smaller than he would have liked. That was something Sinbad had fretted about, but short of having to borrow from moneylenders, he had no other way of handling it. He did not want to finance his experiment through friends, who would expect not only results, but a cut of the profits. He paid for everything out of his own purse, and owed no one a single dinar.

By full dark, nothing had happened, nor had anything occurred on the first two watches. He fell asleep with troubled thoughts just before the middle of the night, after tossing and turning in frustration. Ah well, even if the money was gone for naught, they'd still find some excitement elsewhere. He had plenty of inexpensive trade goods aboard: colorful beads, silk cords, bundles of cloth and leather, and teas. Certainly some far flung land would gladly barter for those!

Still his sleep was restless. Just before dawn, he was wide awake again, and as was his habit, he strode on deck to peer out at the sunrise. Another day was ahead, and they were rapidly moving out into the ocean. Perhaps they needed more room around them for the devices to work.

Even adventurous captains need their sleep. The first few days at sea, Sinbad barely left the deck long enough to have a bite to eat, and when he came back he stayed to watch the sun setting, and then the stars peeking out of the darkened sky. If a light was going to shine, it would show best at night. Yet day after day went by with no sign that the devices were going to activate, and Sinbad grew sleepless with pacing the deck most of the night. During the daylight hours, he kept to himself, personally guiding the ship and ignoring the fretting of Omar, the curious looks of his other boon companions, and the grumbling of the crew.

Sinbad appeared far more ragged each day, with all the sleep he was losing, and he felt far wearier than ever before. After the first full moon began to wane, he knew he was in trouble, and so he fervently hoped for a sign that he had not thrown away his time and money on a hoax.

It was Ralf who inadvertently discovered the secret to activating the devices.

After purposely challenging his frustrated friend to a drinking contest that only the giant Viking was destined to win, he had forcefully suggested that a haggard and stumbling Sinbad leave the deck and go get some sleep. Tishimi and Henri steered the well-inebriated captain to his cabin, and saw him safely to bed, already snoring by the time his head hit the pillow. A habitual early-riser, the female samurai returned to her own quarters to sleep, while Henri rejoined his hulking companion on deck.

Ralf stood at the port bow railing, gazing out into the night and sighing unhappily. Somewhere in the night, Haroun played the set of wooden pipes the Viking had taught him to make, and while the tune was one of the boy's own, the sound of the instrument hearkened back to the big man's youth. Alcohol and inactivity was a combination that always left him feeling melancholy, and this night he was already feeling a bit wistful for the Viking life he'd left behind.

"You had to give that boy something noisy!" Henri said with disgust as Haroun hit a high note that could have fractured stone. "He is always singing as it is, and now he can whistle like a bird. If this voyage is long, I shall go mad, listening to that sound!"

"Is Sinbad asleep?" Ralf rumbled to the far smaller man as the Gaulish archer slipped up beside him.

"Yes, at last. He is taking this disappointment far too hard. We should just forget about these contrivances," he swept an arm gracefully out toward the figurehead, "and just go seek our fortunes as we always have."

"Bah, we need a proper destination. There's too many soldiers in the cities along these shores to go looking for adventure. I don't see us heading anywhere right now where there's a chance of making some decent coin," Ralf added with disgust, "And far too many local pirate boats on the water to have any hope of hanging on to what we find."

He turned toward Henri, and fixed him with a glittering stare. "Up north I know where there are good places to do some raiding. Go inland on the rivers and there are all sorts of villages to plunder. You'll come back with your share of women, farm animals, gold jewelry..."

"Well, I for one am not interested in hauling home sheep and pigs," Henri said with distaste, his arms crossed on his chest.

Ralf laughed uproariously, and slapped him on the back. "I don't know how you can say that with a straight face, my lecherous little friend, for I have seen some of the women you bed, and there's not much difference!"

Henri spat over the side in disgust and remained silent, leaving a morose Ralf alone with his thoughts. Thinking about the life he had left behind while still under the influence of the strong drink brought on a wave of homesickness. The brawny Norseman craved action and adventure, and the past turn of the moon had been extremely dull. He started reminiscing about his homeland so far away, where the snows lay deep in the winter, and recalling how the North Sea was such a captivating but frigid and dangerous mistress.

Haroun's serenade to the stars had died out as the boy sought his own slumber. A ballad came to mind, the words half forgotten, but as he hummed the tune, the verses were found. Ralf lifted his voice into the night, and while his deep baritone was quite rough, it had a heartfelt mournfulness to it for a land of fire and ice left behind.

As the night wore on, a sleepless Henri had wandered over to the port side of the bow and stood brooding on where they could go to find a profitable adventure without getting themselves killed. Unlike Tishimi, who lived frugally and only spent a small portion of her take from each voyage, or Ralf, who at least intended to save more than he spent, the Gaul born archer was a flamboyant man who squandered his money and started each new journey broke again. It took plenty of coin to impress the highly paid courtesans and noble ladies he was fond of wooing, and toward the end of each layover, he could afford no more than a pallet in a poor inn and the occasional dockside doxy as a bed warmer. Several times he had been chased back to the ship by irate landlords or angry whoremongers who had not been compensated properly. It was Sinbad who invariably paid them off, and then deducted the amount from Henri's portion of the next journey's take. Henri never wound up any richer or much poorer than he had ever been, but he still held onto the dream of one day returning to his country wealthy enough to be a fine lord with a large estate and many loyal retainers.

A fog rose around them, obscuring all but the sky. Henri lingered nearby in a gloomy mood, and Ralf's sorrowful-sounding vocalizations weren't helping lift it. When a couple of loud and rather dramatic sighs didn't quiet the Norseman's gravely chant, he turned to say something scathing about rude people who only sing in foreign languages, but instead stopped and stared with unbelieving eyes at an incredible sight that was visible for just a moment through the misty air. Henri bounded a few steps farther forward, and swinging himself up on the gunwale, he hung onto rigging, peering off into the darkness.

Dual frosty blue beams of mystical light shone from the mermaid figurehead. They played out over the rippling waves ahead of the bow, dancing off the crests of foam and froth. Whenever the ship heaved up they illuminated a half visible scene shrouded by a lighter drift of fog that was twisting around the bow. At the farthest reach of those coupled rays, there were glimpses of a distant sunlit vista that even sharp-eyed Henri could just barely make out; though he saw enough to understand it was unlike any continent or island that he had previously traveled to. This was a frozen land of winter, dominated by towering glaciers brooding above lowland steppes, and dotted with great beasts that the long-time hunter had never seen before. Henri's mouth was open and his tongue was too dry to speak as he tumbled backwards into the bow and then scrambled to his feet again. He grabbed hold of Ralf, tugging at his arm and pointing wordlessly.

Ralf was cut off abruptly in the midst of the 17th verse of an ode to the lonesome wanderers of the frigid North Sea. He spun around irritably, but he did follow the direction of Henri's jabbing forefinger. His eyes brightened and he exclaimed, "Holy Odin Hanging From Yggdrasil, that has to be one of the Nine Worlds!"

Henri had no idea what he was talking about. "Well certainly it has to be some world, but I doubt it is one we know. We must wake Sinbad!"

Ralf shook his head. "Why bother? We're still a long way off, and he's drunk and overtired. Let him rest for now. We'll keep watch, and if anything important occurs, we'll wake him immediately. What could possibly go wrong that you and I could not handle?"

Plenty! Henri was thinking, but did not say, for he hated to be chided about being a coward for what he thought of as being appropriately cautious. He drew his jerkin close around him and raised his hood as he took the port side watch in earnest, for just the brief glimpses of such a cold and forbidding place gave him the shivers. The lights wavered as the boat crested waves and fell into troughs, and the scenes ahead flashed in and out of sight. It was a wondrous yet unnerving spectacle, as the great hulking beasts moved about on a snow dusted plain well below the colossal height and breadth of blue-white walls of packed ice.

As night became day, the Blue Nymph drew closer, and the air around them became biting. Already, half-awake men on the decks behind them were shouting and pointing, scrubbing their eyes in disbelief as the night pilot was doing his sleepy best to guide them between scattered ice floes, some of which were sizable, and a few held strange creatures the men had never seen before.

"Somehow, I do not believe this is going to be one of our easier trips," Henri said with an edge of apprehension as dawn crept over the horizon.

"Good!" growled Ralf, and then he gave a hearty laugh. "I was getting bored anyway." An apathetic Norseman could get himself into all sorts of mischief, usually drinking too much, and picking fights over nothing, threatening people with sharp blades, and just making a general nuisance of himself.

Tishimi had taken to her hammock shortly after Sinbad was carried off to bed. She always slept soundly on nights when she had no watch, though a moment's notice could wake her, ready to fight or accompany a shore party. She rose each day before dawn to greet the sunrise and meditate. Coming on deck, she noted the fallen temperature immediately, and that the scenery ahead was incredibly unfamiliar. She almost bumped into Omar on his way up as she hustled back down to rouse Sinbad.

"What in the name of Allah is this unwholesome sorcery?" the crew master exclaimed unhappily as the icy bite of the wind off the glaciers ahead hit him, eliciting a bout of shivering. "How can we have sailed into a frozen world in just one night?" He ignored Henri's fantastic-sounding explanation as he stomped on deck fuming, and harangued the night crew and pilot over an hour for being careless idiots who had put them off course.

A well-rested Sinbad and Tishimi soon joined Ralf and Henri at the bow, marveling at the ocean and land ahead.

"You see? Our nymph has been hard at work all night," Henri said proudly, as if the mermaid figurehead was an actual member of the crew.

"I do! This is amazing!" Sinbad commented eagerly, his face wreathed in smiles as he studied the land lying before them. In the dawn's light, the beams originating from the crystalline tips of her ample bosom were paling, but they could all see plainly that they had entered some sort of arctic area. Always prepared, Omar had broken out woolen cloaks and leather boots used for exploring mountainous areas, which Haroun and Rafi helped distribute amongst those of the crew with the most exposure.

"I see that we will need special equipment for this landing, if we are to go ashore," Sinbad said thoughtfully. "Do you think we can prosper here though?"

"Looks like excellent hunting," Ralf said enthusiastically, and slapped Henri on the back.

"Yes, but under what conditions? It is cold enough to freeze your ah... eh..." Henri glanced sideways at Tishimi, expecting a rebuke, "Your twin furry companions off, while out there," the Gaul archer said with speedy discretion, expecting to be misunderstood in his attempt to censor his comment.

Ralf laughed at his discomfiture. "That might actually slow you down a while—that is, if you had any." The smaller man glared and moved aside.

"I doubt it would affect him," Tishimi said with an arch glance in Henri's direction. "He would likely grow a second set, as a shark does with lost teeth." She was learning to become less reserved and more amicable with her erstwhile brothers-in-arms. Henri did no more than sputter, for he was at a loss for a retort.

"That's enough of this subject for now my friends," Sinbad warned them, though he too was smirking. Rafi had just come forward with warm wraps for them all.

"For now, wrap yourself up well, for the wind grows raw, and with too much exposure, you will chill and become sick with fever and catarrh," Rafi explained as the others shook out the cloaks they had been handed.

"Heh!" Ralf scoffed, though he did throw the cloak over himself, which on the big man with the broad shoulders, looked more like it had been designed for a child. "A sniffle is the least of your worries out there." A big arm was flung wide, indicating the scenario ahead. "When that ice wind off the glaciers hits you, any exposed skin will freeze and blacken. We're going to need leggings and mitts, fur parkas and boots with good soles."

"So it will not be easy to travel inland here without proper clothing. Perhaps we can trade for such things," Sinbad suggested.

"If there are any people in this land; yes, I would think so," Ralf answered eagerly. "Unless of course it is the land of the gods, in which case, we'd need a sacrifice to insure our survival."

"I think perhaps we should go home now," Henri said unhappily. While he had been mesmerized half the night by the land before him, by daylight it reminded him far too much of the alpine areas of his own country, which had claimed many a hunter's life due to falls or exposure—and that land had only normal size beasts. This one seemed to be filled with gigantic long haired creatures that he would have never believed possible, and the glaciers towering over it appeared insurmountable.

Tishimi's thoughts echoed his own, though she did not shrink from the idea of going ashore.

"This is somewhat like the coastal mountains of my country, where snows lie deep in winters, but we do not have those incredible walls of ice. I do see that the area before them down to the shore has some grass and vegetation, so that at least will be traversable and somewhat more temperate. If we can find a safe place to land, we could at least explore it." She seemed almost eager to see the area up close.

"That settles it in my mind. Omar!" Sinbad called back to his shivering and unhappy first mate, "Set us a safe course to bring us as close to shore as we dare. We shall take one of the small boats out, for I am eager to see where our lovely lady has led us."

After a cold meal of olives, dates, ship biscuit, and dried fish, Sinbad, Ralf, Tishimi, and Henri, along with a couple of crewman who would be bearers for trade goods and food, set forth in one of two small boats that was usually kept aboard for excursions in places where there was no dock. Bundled up in woolen capes and quickly assembled winter outfits, with sturdy boots designed for hiking in rough terrain, they rowed the tiny vessel around rocks and ice chunks, heading for a stretch of pebbly beach that was flat enough to land on, sheltered within two headland promontories.

As they drew closer to the shore, the first thing that everyone noticed was that the frozen mass of glaciers were actually quite far off, though an ice field spreading out from them went all the way to the distant coastline and there was some sea ice well out into the open water. Spurs of rocky land dusted with snow rose steeply in the foreground, but the crescent of cold and low shoreline ahead was the only accessible spot. From the ship they had observed fresh water rivulets that resembled small rushing streams as they flowed out to sea, either dropping over cliffs as thin falls with long icicles bordering them or creating wide and shallow deltas, making the water near their landing point rather brackish. There were spouts of steam in spots—*hot springs* Ralf named them, explaining that the molten dragon fire beneath the earth worked its way up toward the surface and the ice became pools of meltwater so warm that a man could soak in barely clothed.

"Perhaps we should look into that," Henri said eagerly. Tishimi rolled her eyes.

"Another time," Sinbad told him. They had come seeking their fortune, not to lie around like harem girls.

"Some of those heated waters will actually spout skyward from the pressures below," Ralf said to their wonderment as they poled the boat in with their oars on the shallow bottom. "Like a great scalding waterfall. If you are lucky, you will see a rainbow in the steam. "It's an omen of good fortune."

"A magical land of fire and ice," Sinbad said reverently as his indigo eyes scanned the vista ahead. Once again he was glad he had pursued the formula for the etheric navigation devices that had led them here.

Ralf was the first one to jump out once they hit sand and grit, and he did most of the work of pulling the boat in once the others had disembarked. He seemed right at home in that harsh environment and eager to be off exploring.

"Where do we go now?" Henri asked, shading his eyes against the glare off of snow and ice. "I see some caves against the walls ahead, but nothing I would want to enter without a torch."

"We need to head upland," Ralf rumbled, but then he stopped and glanced at Sinbad, realizing it was the captain's place to speak, and not his.

"You're the expert here," Sinbad said with a shrug.

"Well," Ralf began again, more thoughtfully this time, "Where we head

There were spouts of steam in spots…

once we're up there really depends on what you want."

"First thing we need to do is trade for more appropriate clothing," Sinbad suggested. Ralf nodded.

"In that case, pick a clear stream, follow the water inland, and you'll eventually find a settlement. People always live near a source of clean water, and they follow the game trails back into the hills and plains to hunt. If we're going to trade, we need to find their villages."

"What if these people... they are not friendly?" Henri asked.

"Then they'll find us first," Ralf said with a pat to the top of his axe. He'd left his sword on board the Blue Nymph, figuring he'd have more use for the double-bitted head of the chopping weapon.

Henri looked more than a little uneasy, and Tishimi sighed and shifted her swords to a more accessible position. The gesture was not lost on them. They were strangers in a land that had obviously never known much in the way of civilization, and there was no telling what manner of savages might live here. Even Sinbad looked around warily. They could very well face attack from the natives.

"Everyone remain alert. We are trespassing in the land of others, so be careful what you do, and stick together! We don't want anyone getting separated and lost."

The slope down to the beach seemed gradual, but the hike up the steep and rocky incline was still a formidable undertaking. There was a lot of erosion, and rock and soil slipped underfoot, so they were forced to go slowly. Eventually they found a well-worn trail of sorts that meandered uphill at odd angles, taking advantage of natural features that made ascending or descending less dangerous, though still tiring. It was narrow, so they trudged single file with Ralf bringing up the rear, and it took almost two hours to reach the summit of the cliff.

"This is no game trail," Henri warned them. "It was made by men to access the beach, likely for fishing and shellfish."

Sinbad looked up, squinting in the daylight glare. "I don't think they are nearby right now."

"No, the water, it is very cold in this season," the little archer from Gaul commented.

"It's filled with ice—that's cold in any season," Ralf boomed from the rear.

They crested the top one at a time, and stopped to reconnoiter.

What had appeared to be fields of snow from a distance were actually steppe-like grasslands that stretched on toward forested tracts. They were dusted with the patchy snow of late winter, but much of the vegetation was uncovered and freshening. The land teamed with wildlife of the most fantastic sort—gigantic beasts that roamed in great herds, many of them shaggy haired and towering over the lush plant life. Flocks of birds filled the skies as they flew up from wallow ponds and the streams that fed them.

Here near the ocean, the air temperature was not as fiercely cold as they had feared, but the wind held a bite that made them grateful for the warm wool and thick leather. The land directly ahead was mostly scrub and grass, still packed with pockets of snow. It also might hold predators of unknown species or dimensions.

"We must remain alert at all times," Sinbad commented as he glanced around, squinting in the bright sunshine off the whitened landscape. "With the size of some of some of these creatures, whatever preys on them must also be huge." The Blue Nymph's well-traveled captain had seen many strange sights and had battled monsters in foreign lands, and he had learned to trust his instincts about what might lie ahead in waiting for a tasty human to wander too close. Already he had noted a pack of what appeared to be heavy-bodied wolves stalking a herd of some sort of giant deer that had spreading antlers like plows with up-swept tines at the ends. These behemoth herbivores stood at least as tall as giant Ralf at the shoulder alone.

Sinbad watched in awe as the pack of six canines raced toward the herd with the intention of cutting out a straggler, and some of the larger bucks turned to defend their does. They did finally isolate a slower moving buck toward the rear, and while the main body of the pack kept the defenders at bay, two of the Dire wolves snapped at the head of the intended target, just missing being swept aside by its huge palmate antlers. While they worried it from the front, one of them slipped up behind it and hamstrung the creature, so that it could not run. The unfortunate victim bellowed in agony as its hindquarters collapsed, and it went down beneath a tumult of rending jaws and ripping teeth that soon bloodied the snow patches around the feebly jerking body.

"You see how they do this?" Henri commented gravely. "Their strength is in how they work together as a team. Even such a majestic beast can be overcome by treachery. What cannot run away, can be killed far more easily."

"That is a brutal way to die," Sinbad said as he watched in awe and disgust.

"Such is the law of the wild," Henri said in agreement, for as a hunter, he understood such things. "All things wish to live, and one creature's death brings more life to others."

"You are far wiser than you let on my friend," Sinbad said quietly, and clapped a hand on the shoulder of the smaller man as they strode forward again.

There was a ponderous group of what appeared to be long-haired elephants moving just beyond the heaving and tearing bodies of the Dire wolves and their kill, the outermost creatures turning to glare at the scenario playing out, their huge lengths of curving tusks spreading out like the transverse ribs of a ship.

"What in the name of Allah makes a creature grow so large?" Sinbad wondered aloud.

"The gods will it so," Ralf answered with surety. "This has to be Nilfhiem, the frozen land of the Frost Giants."

"Such nonsense! More likely, they become huge because they have lush feed year round," Henri contradicted him. "You see all those grasses?" He pointed out toward the plain. "That is excellent grazing. Animals grow big and strong on such bounty. The water comes down from the glaciers and keeps it irrigated. The snow protects the roots in the winter. It is a good system."

"I have never seen so many massive land-bound creatures before," Tishimi said in awe. "My concern is that if there are men here, are they also as tall and broad?"

"Most likely," Ralf said with a laugh. "At least I won't have to stoop to go into their houses!" Ralf was always banging his head on door frames and other overhead structures. He could not picture anyone larger than he was, for even amongst his own people, he had been considered huge.

"Not all things that prosper need be gigantic—not if they are skilled and careful," Henri reminded them, and no one was sure if he was referring to the Dire wolves or himself.

"So says the little man who is the biggest braggart I know," Ralf said with a chuckle, which was echoed by their two bearers.

"Perhaps it is because I actually have something worth bragging about. After all, surprisingly large gifts can be bundled into small packages," Henri countered as he tilted his head down toward his leather trousers. Ralf busted out laughing, shaking his shaggy blonde hair around in disbelief.

"You two are no different than those animals out there," Tishimi said with disgust as she pushed past them. "You would be better off minding the handiness of your weapons than comparing your private parts."

"I think she finally admitted we are well-equipped," Ralf countered, and the men shared a grin. Teasing Tishimi was something they both enjoyed.

Sinbad's mind was on other things besides the usual banter. "Such ivory as those creatures bear... A hold filled with that would be worthy of a Caliph's treasure room in gold," he commented, his eyes riveted on the massive brown-pelted pachyderms.

"Killing such a creature to take its tusks will not be so easy," Henri warned him. "That hair is thick, and I should think they have a quite tough hide beneath it. There is little for trees that I could make a stand in, and I would not want to be on the ground if one of them decided to charge me!"

"Bah, you worry too much—there's a fortune to be made here!" Ralf looked at this place as a challenge worthy of his prowess. Henri, however, seemed spooked by it, for while he had been a capable and knowledgeable hunter, he knew such beasts would not be readily brought down.

Always the eager adventurer, Sinbad took charge. "This day is well underway, and unless we locate a village soon, we'll have wasted the trip. Let's get moving and see what we can find. Ralf, you lead on. Henri and Tishimi, bring up the rear—eyes and ears open. Let us see what sort of people live here, and then I will concern myself about how rich we could become."

Omar had watched the small boat until it disappeared around the bend of the first promontory. He shivered in the unaccustomed cold, which even the heavy wool cloak did not completely shut out. The watches were shorter, and deck work had split into half crews, so that men could go below and get out of the ice wind that continually swept down upon them. Some of the rigging had become slippery with frost, and the deck was treacherous to walk on at times from the continual spray.

The squat man grumbled to himself as he stomped back and forth, beating his arms to warm them. The continual piping and droning in the background from Haroun was not helping his mood. The shrill sound seemed to go right through his head. He looked up at the crow's nest and shook his fist before calling out an order.

"You—Monkey! Must you continually make noise? Put those infernal squawking pipes away, or I swear I will shove them someplace the sun does not shine," he threatened. There was instant silence. Of course that just allowed the howling of the wind to become more noticeable.

Omar was in a foul mood already. He and Sinbad had parted unhappily once more. They had argued back and forth about staying here, right up until just before the exploration party left.

"Sinbad, this is not a place for men such as us," the burly little mate had complained bitterly before the captain went down the rope and bamboo ladder to his boat. "We are not meant for this climate!"

Sinbad had just flashed him the usual 1000 dinar smile and chuckled. "Don't be such an old woman Omar. We've faced worst than this and come out richer than ever before. Besides, you get to remain aboard. We're the ones going out there braving the weather and the dangers to see what this land has to offer."

"You are so kind, my Captain; to allow me to remain behind and stand out here on this open deck with no fire, and freeze to death in such comfort," he had retorted as Sinbad disappeared over the side. "Well, I cannot promise the Blue Nymph will be here when you get done playing around out there. We might just become another big block of floating ice!"

"Then we will tow you home, and thaw you out again, to the delight of your many children who suffer from the heat," was the whimsical answer he got. Sinbad was not concerned about being abandoned, because he knew Omar was loyal to a fault. The ship would still be waiting when they came back.

One of the things that worried Omar now was the amount of broken chunks of ice that gradually came on with the ebbing tide. A growing field of ice floes was building between shore and ship, and it all seemed to be headed their way. Some of them were large enough to capsize the ship if they were jostled up against it. Even without the ice floes, the sea around them bobbed with huge chunks the size of ships. Most of them appeared to be bigger beneath than what showed on top. If they had to retreat because of danger from the ice floes, night would be the most treacherous time of all to make passage. He would have to make a decision about that soon.

"A curse on your etheric navigation devices, for dragging us here where we will likely die of the cold and ice!"

The shore party had followed a stream back toward its source, and were trekking along a well-worn trail as it began to snow lightly. Deeply grooved in spots, it passed through a somewhat rolling upland area of scrubby, windblown trees and boulders dotted with patches of half-melted snow. There was still no indication of recent human habitation, though it was obvious that someone had lived in the area. There were occasional signs of old butchering sites with fragmented bones left close to round hearths that had smoke-blackened remains of drying racks for meat.

"How do they kindle a fire out here without any wood or steel?" Sinbad wondered aloud.

"There are ways," Ralf rumbled thoughtfully. "You carry tinder and a fire drill or bow. A good man can have a small blaze going in minutes." The Viking was from a cold land and he understood the importance of fire. Lives often depended on it.

"Well, at least they have plenty of flint here!" Sinbad commented. Chips and flakes had often lay discarded nearby each hearth.

"You see this?" Henri said, holding up a handful of the stony bits. "This is from tool-making. These people are backward savages. This means have no metals." He let them sift through his fingers and then stooped again to pick up a broken-off section of very straight stick. It was charred on the far end, but still intact enough to show a blunted stone spear point wrapped in sinew. "These are the camps of wandering hunters, because this was a game spear that was damaged beyond usefulness." He looked around them. "These bones are huge! Such men will also be strong and uncompromising. They might be dangerous enemies."

"Whatever has been chewing on these bones will be even more so," Ralf rumbled as he indicated teeth marks and splintered ends that had been broken for what little marrow the hunters hadn't eaten. "You can't blame people for being wary where there are meat eaters the size of horses."

"That is debatable," Henri began, "Men who live with such danger should learn to band together for the better of–"

"Something is coming this way!" Tishimi interrupted, and they instantly fell silent. Of all of the party, she had the most acute hearing.

Still in the distance, but rapidly growing closer, came a high-pitched and quavering scream of terror, along with the thundering sound of a heavy body at a full gallop. The pattering whirl of snowflakes coming down grew heavier, creating a fog of white that was hard to see through. The commotion was moving cross-slope, and generally in their direction.

"Off the path!" Sinbad ordered, and everyone ducked behind rocks for shelter. As the sounds grew near, a short and squat-looking woman with stringy, dark hair and wearing loose furs as clothing came racing toward them through the snowburst, cradling a big-eyed infant in one arm and holding some sort of pointed stick in her unoccupied hand. She was the source of the screeching. Directly behind her galloped a huge grunting and snorting behemoth—a woolly rhinoceros. Spangled with new snow, its late winter coat hung in matted strands that were peeling and shedding, its long, curving front horn held down low as it pounded along.

While the bearers drew back in fright, Sinbad, Ralf, Tishimi, and Henri never hesitated. They had fought monsters together often enough as a team to be able to function without words.

As brave as she was, Tishimi understood that her light swords were no use here, but she had the gift of speed, so she raced out and grabbed at the woman, flinging her out of the way, and distracted the beast long enough to turn it away before dancing off into the now heavier snowfall. As massive as it appeared, the woolly rhino was incredibly fast, and it changed directions with only a little sliding. If not for Ralf racing out like a giant ghost of winter and whacking it hard on the head with his great axe, it would have impaled and crushed her. As it was, the hide and hair was so tough, his axe blade deflected. He only managed to lop off part of an ear, which bled down into an eye. The hairy behemoth stopped to bellow and stomp the ground before tossing its head and charging sideways at a rapidly retreating Ralf.

Henri, from his cover of a tumbled block of stone, leapt up and with the sticky flakes blowing in his face, got off a couple of quick shots—one which stuck loosely in the great humped shoulder, and the other above the affected eye. Neither was more than a bee sting to drive the creature even madder. It shook its head and made a noise somewhere between a snort and a rumbling growl, circling quickly between its two-legged opponents.

Sinbad had secured the woman and her babe behind one of the stones with their bearers, signing to her to be silent, before he stalked out with his trusty curved blade in hand. He was brave beyond most men, but he was also wise in the ways of great creatures, having fought many monsters in his travels. Sinbad understood the futility of using his scimitar against so large and thick-hided an opponent—one that could move very fast and trample or gore him before he could get in a crippling blow of any kind. There would be no sense in getting himself killed due to false bravado.

"We must take this thing down Ralf, or it will chase and kill us one by one," he said quietly, as the beast began to turn toward him. The footing was getting a big slick. Someone was going to fall if it went on much longer. "Tishimi, you and I are the distractions!" he shouted as it came hurtling in his direction full tilt, its nostrils flaring and tiny eyes red-rimmed with fury. Sinbad skipped out of the way, and wove off behind it, making it turn abruptly again. He barely outran it before gaining the cover of a boulder to catch his breath.

Ralf raced back in as the fleet Oriental girl danced lightly into the open, shouting and waving her blades around in a complex pattern, which cleaved the snowfall in dervish-like spins. The woolly rhino caught sight of her, and snorting, changed directions swiftly. Tishimi raced fleet-footed past Ralf, who with a similar grunt and great heave of his own massive body sunk the axe head into the hump not far from where Henri's first arrow had struck. He had been aiming for the head, but the wily creature had tossed up that great curving horn and nearly caught the big man in the chest. Ralf had to jump sideways at the last moment to avoid being gored or trampled and he slid, and so his blow glanced off and struck high. The haft of his axe was ripped from his hands as the head of the weapon sliced into fat and grated on bone, but the wound bled little and did nothing to hamper the enraged monster. It chased him around the stones, looking for a chance to flush the big man into the open and trample him to death.

"It just won't give up! Why is this thing so blasted angry?" Ralf shouted as Sinbad raced in to distract it so that the Viking could retrieve his fallen axe before it was covered in snow, and set up for another blow.

"It is a bull, and this is likely their breeding season, so it is being territorial," a half-visible Henri said coolly. He had nocked another arrow and was sighting carefully over his sheltering stone, his bow canted somewhat sideways so as to have the room to get off a clean shot. He was frustrated at having to follow the erratic movements of the hulking beast through the veil of falling precipitation. A killing hit on such a large creature meant precisely placing the shot in an eye or possibly up inside the mouth, to hit the brain and drop it fast. It was too heavily coated to hope for a heart or lung shot. A gut injury might eventually stop it, but in the cold air it would bleed out slowly, and such a large creature would not lose strength fast enough.

They had to immobilize the beast. His hunter's mind went back over an earlier scenario.

"Sinbad, we are doing this wrong! We must hunt as the wolves do!" Henri called out, recalling the pack that had brought down the gigantic deer.

Sinbad was always quick to grasp an idea. "I had not thought of that—yes, of course!" their dauntless leader said eagerly, with that gleam in the eye he always got as a challenge presented itself. Their situation was already perilous, for with the snow coming down thicker and faster, and the afternoon rapidly passing while they fought the beast, the time of cold darkness—which would no doubt filled with predators which could see far better than they could—would be upon them before they found adequate shelter.

They had to try it, though it would be a matter of timing if this plan of Henri's worked or got them all killed. Those who distracted it would have to get extremely close to the furious creature in order to keep it too occupied to notice someone slipping up from behind. At the first prick, the beast would attempt to wheel around to face its tormentor. It was a dangerous game at best with such a huge and powerful adversary, but Sinbad El Ari was not a man who shrank from danger.

"Tishimi and I will have to take the lead positions for this to work. Henri, you be ready for whatever clear shot you might get. Ralf, back off for now and work your way behind it before you charge in again," he called over breathlessly, for Sinbad himself had just barely raced out of the way of that massive body hurtling in his direction, after agitating the creature enough to get it to leave Ralf alone. He'd slipped twice in the wet snow covering the ground, and barely stayed upright the second time. "We'll keep it confused and hopefully in one spot. We've got to cripple those hind legs."

"Understood!" the Viking rumbled, hefting his axe and angling away through the drifting curtain of snow well to the rear before taking a runner's stance. He was used to meeting an oncoming enemy head on, so it had not even occurred to him that he could do more damage from behind one.

No one could fault their leader for his bravery or his ability to inspire others to risk their lives for a good cause. As the tall Viking set himself up to race in with axe swinging, Sinbad and the small Samurai worked in tandem to keep the enraged beast from moving around as much. Neither could do much damage without endangering their own lives, but they made a good show of running in and feinting back again. Both were light on their feet and moved fast, and their blades flashed as they whooped and yelled in the confused creature's face. The closer they came, the less the woolly rhino advanced, which gave Ralf his opportunity.

Tishimi got a little too close and one flat sweep of the horn knocked her down. She slithered sideways in the wet snow and was back on her feet in seconds, but the creature had lowered its head and butted her down again before raising its front feet to trample her. She made it up to one knee and brought her katana into play, slicing away part of a lip and the outer edge of a nostril before rolling beyond the subsequent charge. The beast bellowed again and turned with her, flinging blood, snot, and saliva, but Sinbad's curved blade was there, slicing into the muzzle of the creature, which backed off with a squeal of pain.

Ralf saw his opening and charged in, the great axe held sideways in his thickly muscled arms and a grimace of effort on his face. He could barely see the bulk of the creature through the blinding snowfall, so he went by feel. The tall Viking heaved his double-bitted blades back and forth, sideways across the upper parts of the hind legs as the beast backed up. It was not as densely furred there, and with the leg muscles tensed, he knew where to cut. On the third swing, the axe went through the hair and hide, exposing the muscles and tendons, which he severed before dodging sideways. He barely made it out of the way as in a splatter of hot blood, both legs buckled and the hindquarters collapsed.

The woolly rhinoceros bellowed in agony as it struggled to get to its feet. Henri left the shelter of his position and came forward until he could see, and then drew back hard on the bowstring. His shot went true this time, up through the eye into the brain case. Ponderously slow, the dying creature's front end dropped with an earth-shaking thud, and it twitched several times before it lay still.

"That was a lot of work, and it took far too long," Henri said as he wiped his snow crusted cloak across his brow rather dramatically.

"For some of us, yes it was," Sinbad countered with a frown. He was exhausted, as was Tishimi and Ralf, for they have been charging through the snowfall and almost continuously in harm's way for over an hour. Henri had bided his time in relatively safe cover, waiting for an opportunity to get off the killing shot. He had not been racing around in slippery footing, trying to outmaneuver a giant beast willing to pound him into mush.

"Well, if I had not reminded you of the way the wolves brought down that great stag, we might still be here come nightfall freezing to death—had we survived at all."

It was true that the wily little hunter had come up with the winning solution. "That was good thinking on your part, my friend," Sinbad added, remembering how the creature's hind parts had collapsed rather quickly once those tendons were severed. "I doubt any of us could have taken it down without your expertise."

Ralf saw his opening and charged in...

"We all do our part," Henri said with a self-satisfied smirk. He cocked his head and peered up at the sky. The snow was lightening as the storm clouds roiled overhead, upper winds pushing it out toward the coast. "Still, we must find shelter soon. We might have no more than an hour or two of daylight left as it is. We will not make it back to the boat safely before darkness falls."

Ralf came over and clapped Henri on the back and he grinned through his blood spattered golden beard. "They will feast us tonight at that woman's village because of our victory," he said with enthusiasm. "You're smarter than you let on."

The unaccustomed praise from Ralf left the small man temporarily speechless. When he recovered his composure, Henri said, "Sinbad, I think we should take a trophy from this beast, if we are to accompany her back to her own people. She does not seem to speak intelligibly, so we will have no idea what she tells them. Perhaps they will be more kindly disposed toward us if they see proof that we saved one of their own."

"A grand idea! Once again, you prove your value to me. Otherwise I'd have turned you away a long time ago for your laziness," Sinbad said with a half smirk, before turning to Ralf. "My large companion, do you think you can chop off that rather prodigious horn and perhaps some fresh meat? If we carry that with us, it should say the things which our language barrier might not."

"It'll take a while, but yes, I can get most of it off," Ralf said with a sigh as he heaved himself back to his feet and shouldered his axe. He came over and looked at the dead creature's head, and then began methodically whacking away at it.

Tishimi meanwhile had gone looking for the frightened young woman and her baby. She was huddled together with the two bearers and their belongings, hiding between several boulders that gave them a modicum of shelter from the battle raging around them. The babe had been nursed and was sleeping, but the woman looked up with a confused mixture of fear and defiance.

"Come," the slight woman in a wool cape over silks and leather armor said quietly as she held out her hands and gestured that the fur clad mother rise.

The frightened woman slowly got to her feet, her gaze unfriendly with lack of trust.

"I will not harm you. I am Tishimi." She said her name slowly several times and patted her chest. Tishimi reached out toward the woman, who flinched and turned aside to protect her infant. Her other hand raised the pointed stick defensively, but Tishimi was quick, and she shoved it downward. "We are not enemies. Tishimi," she repeated one more time with additional emphasis, and then reached out and touched the woman's fur cape, patting her shoulder through it. "Who are you?"

Even with a language barrier, a question makes a distinct sound. Understanding dawned in the woman's dark brown eyes, and they lost some of the wariness. "Myeega," she replied with equal intent, her voice low, harsh, and grating. "Myeega doh Brom!" she pointed the stick back the way she had come when she was running. "Doh Brom!" she said again with great insistence, the look in her eyes fierce and proud.

"Myeega," Tishimi said her name carefully and touched her lightly again, "Tishimi," she said with a smile, patting herself once more. That much about each other they now understood. Tishimi pointed toward the baby.

Myeega snatched the infant away, and Tishimi had to go through the names once more before the other woman understood. She shook her head, a universal human indicator of negativity, and just repeated, "Doh Brom!" and pointed again.

Tishimi nodded and sighed as Sinbad came up. Myeega looked at him with a mixture of awe, curiosity, and fear, with perhaps just a bit of wistful lust.

"You can communicate with her?" he asked Tishimi curiously.

"Only on the most basic level," the Oriental woman answered unhappily. "We have at least exchanged names. Hers is Myeega. The baby's name she would not tell me, or it has none. But she keeps saying something else and pointing back the way she came."

"Probably her clan name or village," Sinbad reasoned, as he motioned their gawking bearers away to go help heft the great chunks of bloody meat that Ralf had finally cut free. Sinbad had some experience in dealing with language barriers. "Myeega," he said, gaining the local woman's immediate attention, ""I am Sinbad. Sinbad," he repeated with greater emphasis, and pointed to himself. She nodded that she understood. "We want to go with you." He slowly put a hand out, indicating the direction she had run from. "Can you take us to your people?" He made a motion that indicated the entire group.

Myeega seemed to grasp what he wanted. She inclined her head and turned to walk away. "Doh Brom!" she said urgently, looking back over her shoulder.

"The day has gotten old, and while the snow has stopped it will be frigid after dark. We need a safe place to stay for the night. We will follow Myeega back to her people, and perhaps take shelter with them," Sinbad ordered.

And so the party started out again.

As the middle hours of the day passed and the feeble sun became shrouded behind clouds, a snow squall came down over the land, veiling it from those on the Blue Nymph. What they could see clearly though was the wind-whipped water around them, in which the twin forces of tide and storm surge were gathering and pushing the ice floes into a solid pack that rapidly advanced on their position. Omar ordered the anchor lifted and the sail partly unfurled, and with the effort of rowers, they eventually had the wind at their back again. That pushed them rapidly away from the shoreline, where they might get blocked in.

"We have turned around!" Rafi said in a surprised tone as he handed Omar a pottery vessel of hot, salted broth made with ice chipped from a chunk that had been hauled aboard and stewed with dried goat and spices over a carefully tended brazier.

"We need to get away from this infernal coast," Omar answered sharply. He did not like being questioned, nor did he care for the company of the intellectual man, who always left him feeling somehow inferior.

"What of Sinbad and his party?" Rafi asked in a more subdued tone.

"He will have to look out for himself," Omar answered with a sigh after a long, warming sip. His fingers and palms were heavily calloused from handling rough and tarry ropes in all kinds of weather, so he did not feel the burn of the thick clay pot. "If we do not move this ship farther away from the shoreline, that sea ice coming will pile up and cause us to capsize." He pointed with his chin back where they had been. "In such cold water, we will all die quickly, and what good will we do Sinbad then?"

"There is wisdom in that," Rafi said in his quiet way. "Yet I wonder how we will find each other later? As I recall, a fog rose around us before we spotted this land, and it is easy for ships to pass each other in such murk. They could become lost to us as well, should they attempt to return."

His words echoed Omar's own troubled thoughts. Still, the safety of the Blue Nymph and her crew were the first mate's foremost responsibilities. Sinbad had proven time after time, he could take care of himself.

Omar was already frustrated and concerned beyond all reason, but a man in charge could show no weakness. So he scoffed aloud, knowing that more than one ear was turned his way. "Stop nagging at me, old man. Go back to your scrolls and do not trouble experienced sailors with your womanish worries. Have you nothing more useful to do? Why not seek a way to keep us from sickness in this wretched cold. Let me run my ship in peace."

Rafi bowed and took his leave as the Blue Nymph began to make her way back out to the more open water. Omar watched the land recede, occasionally giving a rapidly voiced order to the men on the rigging, or those who employed the long oars kept for such times as they could not catch the wind properly. Once the indigo sail fulled and the lines were made fast, the oars were shipped and the sleek teakwood bow began to cut the waves. The fog they had passed through before spotting the snowy vista was now ahead again, and as they began to enter it, both sight and sound of that frozen wasteland and the icy ocean around it receded. Omar whispered a prayer to Allah, and bowed to the east, before facing back toward the hidden land of the north.

I had to move the ship to save it, Sinbad. I hope you will understand why, once you take to your boat again. If that floating carpet of ice came upon us all at once during the night, we would be lost to you anyway. I pray that we don't miss one another on the completion of this foolish voyage!

Myeega led them back along the way she had come. The trail followed a ridgeline just below the summit before it climbed up over the top. It was a long and weary trek just to get back to where she had run into the woolly rhinoceros while out digging roots and tubers with her stick, which she demonstrated for them. Even with the snowfall, the ground torn up beneath the angry creature's great horn and feet showed how fortunate she was to have escaped. She had bolted away quickly and run for her life to avoid it.

About another quarter mile from there, they entered a lightly wooded area. Not ten steps in, Myeega motioned for them to stop, and immediately hunkered down beneath some brush. They followed her example and waited until a small herd of perhaps a half dozen ponderous and long-haired mammoths passed by, on their way over the snow-crusted, rounded hillock to the rocky plain below. Their heads swayed from side to side as long legs shuffled forward in a slow and deliberately swinging stride.

"Such magnificent beasts," Sinbad breathed in a whisper. "Smaller than the savanna elephants of the Dark Continent and far hairier—but those tusks!" He said that last part just a little bit too loudly and Myeega made a shushing noise and slapped his arm.

A big bull stopped suddenly, and turned their way, glaring. He took a couple of tentative steps in their direction, and they froze. More than one set of human eyes was riveted on him. If he charged, they would have nowhere to go but down, and he'd likely catch the slowest of them.

As if to emphasize his claim on his herd, the bull mammoth swung his huge and curving tusks back and forth, scattering the fresh snow while tearing up the grass and scrub before him. Ralf took a good grip on his axe and made ready to spring forward, but Tishimi put a calming hand on his arm. When nothing moved the big beast raised his trunk and tail, urinated a huge stream, and then trumpeting to his cows, he turned and shuffled off again, taking up the rear position where he could watch behind for potential predators.

"That was as close as I ever want to come to such a beast," Henri said in relief once the mammoths were far enough off to dare stand upright again. No one disagreed with him. Ralf stowed his axe and shouldered the big rhino horn again. The two bearers picked up their dripping burdens of slowly freezing meat, and they set off once more.

The mammoth trail was what Myeega wanted. She nimbly sidestepped the wet and yellow snow and leapt past steaming piles of dung, racing down the slope ahead of them.

"Doh Brom!" she called out happily from more than halfway down the pathway, and Sinbad and Tishimi soon joined her. In the dusk below they could just make out a cupped valley with some sort of domed structures arranged around a central pool which steamed lightly in the cold. As they got closer, they could see that the huts were fashioned from gigantic bones and tusks stacked and lashed together, before being covered with hides. Many had small cooking hearths in or near the doorway openings, and there was some sort of central firepit for all who labored at some task to gather around. Fire was everywhere, because in a land of ice, it was the one thing that made the difference between comfortable living with cooked food and bright light, or raw meat and freezing to death in the darkness. Fire lit the darkness that came early in some seasons, and allowed the people to finish their work for the day, or to sit and share tales. Fire kept predators at bay. Without the knowledge of fire, the people living in that ice age land would have died out long ago.

As they grew closer, villagers going about their daily activities stopped to stare at the strangers. Men set down their work and hefted weapons, women and children picked up rocks. A somewhat sulfurous reek tainted the air around them.

"What is this place?" Sinbad said with incredulity.

"Doh Brom!" Myeega shouted again, as if in answer, though she was running far ahead now. Others in similar rough furs came bounding up to meet her.

"I believe it is Paradise, for I am tired of walking, tired of being cold, and my feet are nearly frozen," Henri complained as he came abreast of their leader.

"You see the steam rising from that pool? Their village is built around a hot spring," Ralf called down as he and the bearers followed the others along the path. "My people would do the same thing, for with all that heat coming up from underground, it melts the snow and ice into warmth that takes the chill from weary bones. The snow well away from it is fresh, so it can be melted into clean water to drink and cook with. I should have thought of looking towards the hot springs when we were searching for people to trade with."

"Well, we're here now. Let us go meet the natives," Sinbad said warily, as he tossed back his cloak to expose his scimitar in case the introduction did not go well. Several men in furs and with long tangled hair and beards had intercepted Myeega, and she was vigorously explaining herself in harsh words and expansive gestures. The men were clutching spears, and their eyes went from the excited woman to the advancing party. Most were riveted on Ralf, who towered over everyone else, though a few stole glances at Sinbad, whose dark skin was something they had never seen before.

Sinbad stopped his party just out of reach of their now less casually held weapons, and he bowed lightly.

"I am Sinbad, from over the seas," he said, making a motion of waves and water with his hands and pointing in the direction of the coast. "These are my companions," he added, slowly and gracefully sweeping first one arm and then another out to in one direction and another, indicating his small group should draw together, for they were gradually being surrounded by villagers. There were men of all ages, many women and children, and a few toothless elders. "We have brought Myeega home safely." He indicated the woman who had turned to watch him, having handed off her fussing infant to another young mother, who nursed both her own and Myeega's child.

There was suspicion in their eyes, and the attitude was less than friendly. They viewed Ralf especially with distrust.

"I do not think they understand you," Henri said with an edge to his voice as the ring of men closed in.

"Offer them the meat and horn," Sinbad said quietly, "But make your movements slow and say nothing for now. They are just wary of strangers."

Ralf set down the horn and then pushed it forward with his axe. The bearers each set down their bloody burdens and backed off.

Myeega suddenly turned and called out, "Doh Brom!" and some other things they could not understand. The crowd parted down the middle and a white haired and aged woman with a pronounced limp came forward. She wore a long mantle of fur over her tunic and leggings, and a necklace of bear teeth and claws strung on rawhide. In her left hand was a staff of wind twisted wood topped with tips of branching antlers and a strange looking, flat headed human skull, all festooned with strings of shell and animal teeth that rattled. In her right hand, she thrust forward a primitive carving done in mammoth ivory of a nude and very corpulent female.

All the men around her looked down at the snow, pointed their spear points downward, and murmured a phrase that sounded reverent.

No one in his party knew what to make of that but Sinbad, who in his travels had seen other cultures who were matriarchal. "They want us to acknowledge their icon," he said quietly. "Bow or do something that indicates respect." Everyone inclined their heads and looked down.

The old woman stepped forward and unsmiling, reached out and lifted Tishimi's chin. She glared at the Oriental girl, turning her face from side to side, and asking some sort of question.

"I do not know what she wants of me!" Tishimi said through clenched teeth. The elder woman's frown deepened. Fortunately Myeega stepped forward.

"Doh Brom," she said, indicating the elder woman. "Tuh-shee-mee," she said shoving a finger into Tishimi's chest. She mouthed a few other things too, said so guttural and rapidly there was no chance to even guess what was meant.

"Tuh-shee-mee!" the older woman said slowly, and leaned forward as if to peer into the younger woman's eyes. She bumped foreheads with

Tishimi, three times intentionally, in some sort of ritual. She tucked away the female idol, and indicated the village with a sweep of her arm before taking Tishimi's arm and turning to trod off proudly with her, strung shells and bits of drilled and carved bone tied to knotted anklets on her boots jingling. The invitation was evident. They were to come with her, and would be welcomed.

"I noticed that none of these women looked down when their men did," Henri said as he walked beside Sinbad and Ralf. Men had come forward to take their offerings of meat and horn, and others had fallen in behind them, herding the two bearers along with the shafts of their spears rapped lightly across their legs.

"It is often so where women rule," Sinbad explained. "It this culture men defer to their mothers and wives."

"That is unnatural," one of the bearers, an eager young man named Farhad said. "Men should always make the decisions. Women are too silly and fickle to be trusted."

"That sort of attitude will get you killed here," Sinbad warned him, and the youth went silent.

"They seem friendly enough now," Henri said eagerly, as women along the way came up to stare at these strange, new men with speculative gazes. Some of the bolder ones touched Sinbad, and made what sounded like suggestive comments to him.

"You better be careful to keep your hands to yourself while we're here," Ralf added, looking down at his small companion. "They won't remain friendly if you bed some chieftain's daughter."

"How you insult me! Bedding women is not all I think of!" Henri protested, but Ralf just laughed, and then hushed when the men pressed in closer with their spears. His hand tightened on his axe, but he did not draw it. It was just a misunderstanding.

"Yes, do be cautious my friends, and keep your voices down, because we have a serious language barrier, and we are outnumbered as well. Let us be ambassadors of goodwill this evening. They have shelter and food we will need tonight."

"I do not like this place," their other bearer, a plump man named Saeed complained. "It stinks!"

"The water is full of earth salts that make it smell like rotten eggs. It's good for your skin though," Ralf reassured him. "Besides Saeed, you don't smell very pleasant on your best days," the Viking quipped, and both Henri and Farhad chuckled.

Saeed looked daggers at the tall man's back, but he said nothing more.

This giant Norseman was a powerful fighter with a quick temper, as well as one of Sinbad's favorite companions. Saeed knew he must take the insult without a retort, but he seethed inside, and vowed to get back at Ralf for that someday. The boy Farhad was new and so could be excused for his foolish insolence after a private warning later on, but Saeed had been amongst the crew for several seasons of numerous voyages and felt he should be more respected.

He would have preferred to remain aboard and deal with irritable Omar and his canings when a man was caught sleeping on watch, but Sinbad himself had chosen him to come along, pointing out that he was strong and needed the exercise. Saeed was miserable, for he never enjoyed hiking, and even with the warm woolen cloak and boots he shivered with cold. His feet and back hurt, and he was covered with smelly dried rhino blood from carrying the dripping meat. He had considered the trek inland a waste of time, and now he was convinced the captain of the Blue Nymph was a madman, and was going to get them all killed in this place of monster animals, stinking steaming ponds, and ice-laden winds.

In spite of the snowstorm, it was nearing spring, the season of renewal. The people of the village were still lean from the winter, but hunting lately had been good, though they had lost several men to it already. With the addition of the two haunches of rhino, they were well inclined to lay out a feast for these friendly strangers with the weapons of smooth and shining rock. The travelers were made welcome with an offer of a dip in the hot springs, for which Tishimi was allowed to go first. Not the least bit shy, she doffed her cloak and clothing, and joined women of the village in a long, hot soak which took the chill and weary ache from her bones. Her wool cloak and silks were returned to her, but she was also gifted with a set of fur tunic, leggings, and crude leather boots with thick soles and some sort of soft hair pelts sewn inside. That native outfit was far warmer to wear once she left the comfort of the water and the freezing air hit her skin again. Several women helped to vigorously dry and dress her while their leader looked on, and they explained in gestures and demonstrations how to get in and out of the clothing. There was sort of a flap beneath that tied in place to keep the cold out, but allow normal body functions without half disrobing in a climate that would often cause frostbite on exposed skin.

"Ralf is correct," she told the men of her party as they passed by, being lead down to the rock walled pool. "It may smell horrid, but the water is wonderfully warm and restores the body. It is a marvel of Nature!" She smiled up at the Viking.

"A gift from the gods," he corrected her, but be he grinned back. Tishimi had been always been shy around him, and so they seldom spoke, except in scathing remarks.

"What wonders this world holds for those who seek them," Sinbad said with a sigh, as he sank, naked and gleaming like polished mahogany wood, into the water up to his chin, with a woman on either side to scrub him down with hands full of fine ground pumice. They seemed determined to see if the dark color of his skin was removable. "This is an incredible place. I'd not expected to find such a civilized lifestyle here."

"They are still primitive compared with us," Ralf said with half closed eyes and a satisfied smile as one woman scrubbed his broad and muscular back just where it always itched beneath his leather armor, while another traced old scars on his arms and chest, and ran fingers through a mat of blonde chest hair. A third one sat on a rock nearby, still fully clad while she deftly worked with an antler carved awl and bone needle, pulling sinew to stitch together furs. She was adding on to existing clothing to make leggings and some sort of tunic that would fit the Viking man's oversize frame. Now and then, she would chatter to the other two women, and they would prod him to stand and turn. She would eyeball his naked body so that she knew what adjustments to make. There was a general whoop and some sort of trilling of appreciation from the women every time his big form rose out of the water. They had even gained a few extra spectators amongst the younger and older females of the group, who chattered amongst themselves in an obviously ribald manner.

"Oh do sit back down my oversize friend; you are scaring these poor ladies to death. We have all seen enough monsters today," Henri said with mock concern.

"You're just jealous that the comelier ones prefer me," Ralf said with a laugh. Henri grimaced. He had two bathing assistants of his own, but one was an older woman, gray-haired with sagging breasts and missing teeth, and the other a roundly pregnant middle aged mother of two. They were just as helpful, but not terribly interested in him or he in them.

"Not all of them do," Farhad said with a smile at the slender and rather pretty girl who assisted him and Saeed. She smiled back shyly, and scrubbed him extra hard. He splashed water at her, and she splashed back, both laughing and squealing, until their headwoman frowned and said a sharp word and she stopped.

Saeed spat in the water. "You act like everything is fine, but we do not understand these people! Why does that old hag watch us so? How do you know they are not cannibals?" he said with disgust.

"Because they are cooking us dinner and giving us clothing?" Henri suggested with sarcasm in his voice and rolling eyes.

"That old woman has a skull on her cane, or did you not notice that? They could be washing us clean before we are murdered in our sleep and become tomorrow's feast." Saeed countered.

"That is quite enough from you today Saeed!" Sinbad snapped. "You will mind your tongue while you are here, or lose the use of it."

Saeed gave his captain a curt bow before he pushed the girl away and climbed out clumsily, beating his arms on his flabby chest in the cold air. Two women rushed up to dress him, but he grabbed his things, turned his back on them, and struggled to dress while still half wet, ignoring the village clothing laid out for him. He stomped away shivering to go sit alone by the fire and nurse his anger.

The headwoman looked after him with a frown deepening the wrinkles on her face. She said something in a harsh and bitter tone to the others, who hurried through their ministrations.

"That's enough bathing for now," Sinbad told his people as he gently disengaged the women tending him and stood up. Their eagle-eyed hostess had already risen and left. The other men of his party reluctantly followed suit, and they were rubbed down with hides and then quickly dressed as natives, before being herded back toward the biggest dwelling, where the feast would be held. A great fire had been laid, fed with some sort of white rock that burned hotter and longer than wood, with some surprising crackles and pops as it feel apart. It also gave far more light.

While the others ate, Myeega—her babe well fed, bundled, and asleep— stood before her village and told her story, illustrating key points with her hands and her digging stick. She was very good at acting out what had happened, and with the flickering fire backlighting her, it was as if the unseen parts of the drama were about to come to life through some sorcery of the mind. The spell she spun kept her people enraptured so that questions were infrequent, and their leader pointed the butt of her staff at whoever was allowed to speak next. They were very respectful and did not interrupt foolishly, though one of the mature hunters continually frowned

"You will mind your tongue while you are here…"

at Sinbad and his party, which were now being closely regarded by all their women.

After Myeega's speech, there were several formal speeches of welcome. No one in Sinbad's party understood a word other than their own names, though they learned quickly that a shoulder punch or shove from a man was a sign of camaraderie. That was when Sinbad presented his bundles of beads, baubles, and shining bits, which were well received. A back and forth discussion of sorts went on, with plenty of hand gestures and quickly scrawled signs in the loose sand around the firepit. What the villagers wanted to know was where these travelers were from, and what they wanted.

Sinbad tried to explain his ship and trading, but the people of this cold land did not understand the idea of regular commerce. They had some sort of barter system with other tribes they trusted, and so when he indicated that he desired mammoth ivory, the hunters nodded sagely. The big creatures were not easy to kill, but if these warriors were brave enough to face down a male woolly rhinoceros, they might actually be some help on an early spring mammoth hunt. Plans were already being made for an excursion the next day, since the heavy snows had ended after the last full moon and the thaws were coming. The big creatures had been regularly wandering through on their migration trails from the sparse and arid coastal steppes that provided low quality browse during the winter, to the far more lush plains lands below the glaciers, which were just opening up for the season.

As the evening wore on, most of the village relaxed, and so did Sinbad's party. Even Saeed showed a passing interest in the hunter's dances in costume, though he quietly mocked them to Farhad as godless savages. Some sort of intoxicating liquid was passed around, and the newcomers were urged to partake. Sinbad took an experimental sip, and refrained from making a face at the bitterness before he passed the crude bowl over to Ralf.

"Drink at least a small measure, for we are guests at a feast in our honor," he insisted. All complied except Tishimi and Saeed, and it was only at the man the people frowned. Women did not have to imbibe to touch the spirit world, for they were closer to it already by their gender.

"This seems quite strong," Henri said with more caution in his voice than usual. Even the normally profligate archer had his limits. He took no more than a single sip.

The women of the village had been reserved at first, but once the hunt dances were over, one after another of the mate-less ones paraded themselves before Sinbad and his men, displaying their availability somewhat suggestively. Apparently they believed that some sort of dowry or bride-price had been paid, so each of the newcomers might choose a companion—at least for the evening. This was the people's way of insuring that new blood flowed in the veins of the tribe, for a clan that interbred too often soon had deformed and sickly babies, and friendly strangers were hard to come by where all competed for the same resources.

The headwoman issued some sort of command, and all the women who had offered themselves came forward and stood before them, looking expectantly at these few new men and holding their bellies. The meaning there was clear—*I wish to be with child*. Having been introduced as their leader, Sinbad was asked to rise, and so was given the option to choose for himself.

"I suppose we should not insult them," he said with a wry smile. He picked a particularly attractive woman, one that made the hunter who had been frowning at them scowl even deeper. Other women looked at Sinbad with great longing, but there were not that many who were old enough to please him, and yet were unattached. It would not do to make an enemy by taking another man's mate to bed. She led him off to her dwelling, to the disappointment of many others.

Due to his size, Ralf was handed over to two young widows who were sisters, and they giggled and steered him away to their furs in the hut they shared. Henri was initially offered to the slender maid who had attended Farhad and Saeed, whose name was announced as Afra. She looked longingly at Farhad, and he at her, until the Gaul man sighed and walked her over to the disappointed lad. He removed Afra's hand from his arm, and gently laid it on Farhad's.

"She will be happier with you," he said quietly, and turned away before he could see the joyous looks of gratitude on both faces. His generosity did not go unnoticed. He was surprised when Myeega herself came forward to take his arm. "But you already have an infant!" he protested, and made a rocking motion with his arms. She stomped her foot and boxed his ears before propelling him away.

Saeed refused to look at any woman who stood before him. Someone pushed a scrawny youth his way, and he snarled angrily before he spat into the fire and looked down at his booted feet. Eventually they just left him alone, and he curled up in his cloak by the fireside and was soon snoring.

Tishimi sat near the headwoman on the other side of the fire, and looked around uneasily. Would they force the same sort of carnal decision on her too? She had no desire of male company at that moment, for her favors were something she reserved till the day a true warrior and nobleman of her own degree came into her life. Sinbad was as close as she had come to that ideal, and she would not ruin their friendship with impure thoughts of physical involvement, or the foolish romantic yearnings of a girl. She was Bushi—a Samurai—and held herself to a higher standard than the dainty fleshly body she inhabited would indicate. She shook her head lightly when several young men came forward, and hoped they would understand.

"I cannot take a man," she told the other women around her, though they could not understand her words. "I pray I may be forgiven, but I have promised to be true to my order." She touched her weapons as emphasis.

Fortunately, the headwoman had heard Myeega's tale of how the slim one fought bravely and with grace. She had also been a warrior in her time, and so she understood the reluctance, and did not press upon this female hunter and fighter a chance to mate. A woman who fought alongside men could not become with child or she would be useless for many moons. There were herbs for that, but some women conceived anyway. The headwoman waved dismissively, and the men all bowed and left. Only Saeed snored by the fire, someone having thrown an old ratty fur over him.

"Tuh-shee-mee," she said to get the Oriental woman's attention, and then patted her own chest. "Doh Brom," she said, and some other things that Tishimi could not understand. She pointed to the kantana and wakizashi that had been laid aside, and said something else, which made Tishimi shake her head and sigh. When the headwoman knew she was not being understood, she seemed to stop and think for a moment, and then grabbing a gnawed clean bone off a nearby rock, she pulled a curved flint scraper blade from her belt and carved off the end. Using it like a writing implement, she drew some crude pictures in the sand, and then pulled up the fur of one of her leggings, to show a horrible scar that left the calf distorted and disfigured.

Tishimi studied the pictures and the scar, and then she understood. "You were a hunter," she said, first pointing to the older woman and then mimicking the spear throwing stick figure in the pictograph. "A great beast injured your leg, and the men left you for dead." She pointed to the indication of something large with teeth and claws, the scarred leg, and then a woman's figure laying on the ground beneath the creature, her spear raised in defense. "Yet you did not die—you killed it as it came back for you! You saved many lives," Tishimi pointed to a hunting party of stick figures that were anatomically drawn as men, "and were very brave, though you nearly lost your own life."

"Brom," the other woman said, and she pointed at the men. "Doh Brom," she added, pointing to herself.

"Brom—man," Tishimi said, pointing at the men in the hunting picture. "Doh Brom—not man, woman," she added, pointing to the clan leader sitting next to her, and then herself.

The headwoman's face was wreathed in a smile, and she let the fur fall back over her injured leg. Now they were getting somewhere! She withdrew the female idol and pointed at it and then at Tishimi, indicating those areas of her that were distinctly female. "Doh Brom, Tuh-shee-mee," she said, and covered those parts before bumping foreheads with her three times again.

Doh must mean woman or female leader. "Doh Brom," said Tishimi aloud, and indicated the little carved woman.

The headwoman shook her head in frustration, and put the female idol aside. She drew a picture of an anatomically correct male, and pointed to it and said "Brom" several times to make sure Tishimi understood that 'Brom' did actually mean man. The headwoman looked around before rubbing it out. "Doh Brom," she said again, and then pointed to herself.

Understanding dawned in the younger woman's green eyes. If Brom meant man, then Doh must mean...

"Doh Brom, Tuh-shee-mee," the older woman continued, and pointed to first the rubbed out man, and then Tishimi herself.

That's when Tishimi understood. "Man," she said, pointing to the rubbed out spot. "Brom means man. Doh means no. Tishimi has no man." She made a motion like men walking away, and the headwoman nodded sagely. "Tishimi Doh Brom." That got her an even bigger smile. She bumped heads with the woman named 'Doh Brom'—No Man—three times more and they patted each other's backs, because they were sisters in spirit in a world where female warriors must fight harder than the men around them to earn some respect.

The next day dawned clear and colder. His female companion had left just before sunrise to attend to her tribal duties. When a smiling and still somewhat sleepy Sinbad came out of the hut to relieve himself, he saw that men of the village were making ready for an expedition. Several looked his way and jabbered, obviously joking about what had happened over the course of the night. One was scowling in his direction, and Sinbad noted that.

Ralf was already up and was gnawing on dried meat, washing it down with melt water and wishing that was ale. "As near as I can figure, they're going hunting," he said eagerly.

"Have we been invited?" Sinbad asked, stowing away his scimitar before fastening his cloak over his furs.

"I believe so. They have been trying to get Henri up for a while now, but he is still snoring away like a camel." They shared a grin. If even perpetually amorous Henri was satisfied, Myeega must have incredible stamina for the mother of a young infant—one who had also walked for miles before and after running for her life while been chased by a huge and angry wooly rhinoceros.

"What of the other two?" Sinbad asked, stretching and yawning again before he accepted a strip of smoked meat and a hollowed bone cup of some sort of hot herbal tea from his grateful companion of the night before, who had gained great status in their tribe by being chosen by the brown skinned leader of the strangers.

"Farhad has not been seen yet, and the hide is still down over the opening to his hut, though they have been making enough noise to raise the dead," the Viking said with a short laugh. "That boy has the appetite and endurance of a bull, from the sound of things. Saeed, that lazy son of a swine, is off hiding somewhere. I haven't seen him this morning."

"Then we will leave him to himself, and Farhad as well, unless he comes forth soon," Sinbad insisted, as he watched the hunters making ready. "Wake Henri though, because I would like him to join us, if we are going after the long haired elephants, as I suspect." Always observant, Sinbad had noted that the men readying their spears were rubbing themselves in mud mixed with mammoth dung, and that one of them had donned a cape of long matted hair from the beasts. "I am going to try and speak to the leader of the hunt," he indicated a man with brown braids threaded with silver hairs, "and make sure we get invited along. Give us a few moments alone, and then you can join us," he added before walking off.

"I'll do that. I had planned on going myself, if they'd have me," Ralf answered while heaving himself to his feet. He strode off in the direction of Myeega's hut, and lifting the edge of the flap of hide that kept out the cold, called in loudly, "Ho, my little friend—wake up and get your clothes on! It seems we're going hunting today!"

Henri came stumbling out, bleary eyed and desperately in need of a quiet spot to empty his overburdened bladder. Ralf turned away as he headed for the nearest tall stone. "That woman—she would not leave me alone!" he bragged. "I had no idea these people were so friendly that they would share their wives."

"Not all of them are so thrilled to see us," Ralf cautioned him as they strolled back toward the fire together so that Henri could grab a quick bite of food and fill his waterskin for the day. "See that man over there with the black wolf cape?" Ralf indicated with a subtle thrust of his chin and Henri nonchalantly followed his gaze to where the frowning hunter was arguing with someone else while they watched Sinbad drawing pictures in a snow patch with the head of the hunting party. "He has been giving Sinbad the Evil Eye since we got here. He bears as much watching today as the animals will."

Henri glanced casually in that direction again, but the man was now looking at them. He feigned spitting something to the side, and then took another sip of tepid water. "He does not seem pleased with Sinbad. I would not trust him alone with our captain." He was looking down at the fire again, noticing the same white chunks in it as the one last night, and part of his mind wondered what they were.

"Nor I," Ralf said interrupting Henri's thoughts, "but Sinbad can take care of himself. Ah, but here comes our Farhad. And look, he can still walk!"

The girl clung to him until she was called away to her duties. The two older men took turns teasing the beaming youth until Sinbad motioned the three of them over, and they were shown the plan for the day.

The leader of the hunting party was an experienced man that they learned was called something that sounded like Gorriz. The other hunters seemed to respect his judgment, and deferred to him for how they would handle their quest. With the extra mouths to feed, they had need of fresh meat, and Sinbad had intimated he and his company were quite interested in accompanying them, for he sought the ivory in the tusks of the great beasts. These outland strangers who had saved the life of one of their own had proved friendly and generous, so clan customs dictated that such potential allies should be allowed to ask for a boon.

The men were organized into parties of spearmen and beaters, with Sinbad and Farhad in with the beaters, though Ralf with his superior strength and size was counted amongst the hunters. He was initially given several light spears and a spear thrower, which he accepted, though he expected to use his axe once those were gone. "Bah—these are flimsy things I'd give to a child," he complained, showing how wobbly the spears he had were made by waving one around. "This wouldn't bring down a tame sheep."

"They are made to be thrown with that device," Henri pointed out, as he retrieved his bow and quiver. "Just as an arrow can fly far and go deep, so will those spears."

"I hope so," said Ralf without enthusiasm. "Just glad I don't have to depend on them to hunt these monsters every day."

"Agreed," the small archer from Gaul said as he found his place in the hunting party. "Still you must admire these men for their bravery," he added, as he was joined by a youth with a sling and two other archers with primitive though well designed bows equipped with stone tipped arrows that had no fletching. Their weapons were obviously intended to be used at point blank range—a situation that wily Henri was not entirely comfortable with. He wrinkled his nose in disgust as he spread the smelly dung and mud mixture over himself. "A lot of good bathing does if the next day you are to be smeared with excrement and covered with flies," he complained.

"It will hide your man stink," Ralf rumbled as he casually wiped any exposed skin of his own—including his face—with heaping handfuls. "Keeps the predators away, and the biting insects won't find you so tasty. Besides, the ladies love you no matter how bad you smell. That toothless grandmother looked heartbroken that you didn't wink in her direction."

"Always I am the butt of your jokes," Henri commented with a frown.

"You certainly smell like a camel's rear," Farhad commented as he walked away. Being a beater, he only needed to lightly coat his skin with stripes of mud as sort of a camouflage until they were in place.

"We all will smell worse than this by the end of this day," Sinbad interjected. "Now let us get moving, or we will be left behind like the women."

"Not all women remain behind," a familiar voice behind them said, as Tishimi, dressed in furs and already smeared with mud and dung, came loping up. They had completely forgotten about her in their eagerness to be off. "A small group of women are packing up butchering tools along with some sort of tents, to drag out on skids to where the hunters will be."

"Where have you been hiding?" Henri queried curiously as she accepted a spear and nodded to the head of the hunters. Obviously Gorriz had been expecting her. Her swords were scabbarded at her side as always.

"She must have found a warm bed with someone last night and was reluctant to leave it," Ralf said with a knowing wink, which garnered him a bland glare from the slight woman as she trod past Henri on her way to join the hunters. She stopped and confronted Ralf, and they were comically mismatched, with him so tall and broad and Tishimi quite short and slight, even bundled up against the cold.

"For your information Norseman, I have no reason to hide, nor did I spend the night fornicating in strange furs, as you men did," she stated firmly. "I slept soundly and alone, rose before dawn, and stepped outdoors just in time to see our bearer Saeed raiding their dried meat and filling his waterskin before he set off back the way we had come. I followed him at a distance, and then came back to report that I think he is headed to our boat."

"Well, he can't launch it and row away on his own," Sinbad said from somewhere behind them. "But I will say here and now that this is his last voyage with us. I will not deal with men I cannot trust to obey even simple orders without complaining, or deserters who shirk their responsibilities and abandon their companions. Saeed has had many chances to redeem himself. We will put him off at the next port."

Gorriz looked behind as did several of the other hunters, and he said something gruff and low, making a sign that they were to stop talking and get moving. They began to climb the ridge in a different direction that they had come in from the day before. It was steep and somewhat treacherous footing, and it took enough time and effort in that frosty air that no one was tempted to even whisper. On the far side was a zigzagging trail down through rock and brush cover toward the plains below. The thawing grassland was dotted with great creatures such as they had seen previously, including the tall and long haired mammoths.

Another hour's climb down and they would be on the plains by midday. Then would come the hunt for a straggler amongst the quarry, and the attempt to surround and bring it down would begin.

This was the season when all the migratory plains beasts were on the move toward their spring pasturage. There they would soon drop their calves, and the females would make copious milk for them while feeding on lush and thick forage of the highest quality. Over the warm months they would all fatten into robust creatures that could survive the harsh winters. The people knew this, as many generations of their kind had hunted here.

Others came to hunt as well, both human and four legged predators. While they were descending, Henri happened to look up at the cry of a bird of prey in the distance, and caught sight of another band of hunters slipping low through the brush several miles off. Something about them seemed different—they were shorter, walked oddly, and carried heavier spears, mostly remaining under cover. He understood their tactics as a 'wait-and-see what passes by' approach. One would come home empty-handed most days, hunting that way. Not too far from where they were headed, a big bear emerged from the brush just long enough to sniff the air before it disappeared once more.

Henri did not think to mention these other men to Sinbad until later in the day, for once they were on relatively level ground, the two other archers and the single sling-stone thrower amongst his group were getting their orders, and he had to jog to catch up. As far as he could determine, they were to run in once the beast was cordoned off from the herd and keep it too busy to charge while the spears were taking their toll.

It was going to take many spears to put down one of those immense creatures. If anything, the mammoths had longer and more abundant hair than the woolly rhino did, though Henri and his companions had no idea how thick their hide was. Hitting a vital spot and getting enough penetration to do some damage would be hard. He had no doubt though that Gorriz's hunters would know their business. If they didn't, they would have starved to death long ago. Yet one thing bothered him... in a place so fertile with somewhat smaller game, what was the point of challenging the biggest and most dangerous creatures? Were they only hunting the mammoths to please Sinbad, or did this giant beast of the frozen land have so much use to them, it was worth the additional risks?

Henri knew he would soon find out.

The night aboard the Blue Nymph passed slowly, and most of the crew were solemn and quiet. Without the icy wind, the cold had greatly abated, but the spirits aboard hadn't lifted. Even Haroun did not play his pipes, nor did he sing.

The fog that lay between them and the ice world that Sinbad and his party had left to explore had some dampening effect on their mood, as well as making any sounds bounce back eerily. Many of the sailors aboard were superstitious, and thoughts of jinni or sea monsters creeping up on them through the darkness and murk kept all but the hardiest men awake. Most of the crew had sailed with Sinbad before, and they had seen sights that defied the imagination. So while a regular watch was set, sleepless men crouched on the deck in small groups, waiting to see what would happen in this abnormal buffer zone between the warmer seas they knew well, and that strange, frozen land.

Toward morning, while the sky was still dark and starless and the fog impossibly thick to see very far through, a series of bumps and thumps on the hull of the ship brought half-sleepy men to their feet in fright. Fearing that the floating sea ice had caught up with them, Omar was out of his hammock and on deck in moments. Men stood in small groups, speaking in hushed tones and looking down toward water around them in apprehension.

"What are you—Sindhi sailors, or a Sultan's harem full of concubines squealing over the sight of a mouse? Get this ship moving!" Omar harangued them, though his eyes also went wide with anxiousness every time they felt another thud on the hull. The Blue Nymph was well made but lightly built so as to ride the waves and cut through the water with great speed. Some of those hits rocked her slightly.

"Omar, we are becalmed and have no wind here! We cannot outrun these monsters below," one man complained and he was echoed by others. With the gray light of dawn they could just barely make out dark shapes cutting through the waters.

"Then get busy on those oars you fools!" the stout little man blustered as his reed cane laid into them until men were running for their positions to escape his wrath.

"Haroun!" Omar shouted in a voice that thundered loudly in the echoing silence that was only broken by lapping of waves and men getting to their rowing stations, "Get up in that crows nest, you mountain monkey, and look down. Tell me what sort of infernal beasts these are!" Omar had seen the occasional back fin, but their bodies seemed far too long, dark, and wide to be sharks.

Haroun was climbing the rigging almost before he was awake. Once well up above the deck of the ship, he could just make out the speeding dark bodies of something relatively fish-like, though most were large enough to be a third of the Blue Nymph's length. These monsters were shining black

Night aboard the Blue Nymph passed slowly...

with white patches, and they blew water from their heads as did the far smaller dolphins that often guided them in and out of ports. The young man had never seen such creatures before, and he watched amazed as one of the leapt from the water to fall back splashing.

"What is it Haroun, you useless boy; are you struck dumb? Tell me what you see!" Omar demanded. The Blue Nymph's furious first mate had heard a great splash but in the low light could not quite make out at his level what had caused it. There were mysterious spumes all around the ship, and the bumping and thudding had increased.

"Omar, I do not know how to describe them! They are like huge black and white sharks, but blow like whales, so I think—"

Haroun would have continued, but just then, one of the oarsmen shouted in panic and yanked back as his oar was grabbed in the huge jaws of one of the creatures. The surprised man shrieked in abject terror as he was almost jerked over the gunwale, but two others caught at his midsection and legs and tugged until the paddle end splintered and it was set free. It was pulled up showing toothmarks where a large chunk had been bitten off. That got all the oarsmen jabbering at once, and Omar had to be brutal in his discipline to gain their attention again.

"Allah, why do you hate me so, to burden me with such whimpering babies for a crew? Get back to your positions you fools, or we shall never escape this herd of water demons. Pull for your lives, if you want to go home to your family again!"

Omar had finally seen one of the great creatures breaching, and could verify that the maw of the beast was filled with large and sharp teeth. It was the smaller but extremely fierce killing whale that the old time mariners called Grampus, the white streaked black devil of the sea. The water around the ship boiled with them, and they kept buffeting the Blue Nymph from side to side in an attempt to knock men off her deck. Omar mentally berated himself for ever agreeing to this foolish excursion.

"You see Sinbad?" he muttered, too low for the others to hear, "This is what happens when you play with magic. Allah now punishes us by sending these Jinn in the form of sea beasts to ruin your ship and send those of us who are not eaten down to a watery grave."

They spotted their target for the day, an inexperienced mammoth cow that had just given birth to a premature male calf. The unfortunate little creature had expired after drawing a few shuddering breaths, but it was still slightly warm, judging by the steam rising off its body in the early morning sun. The young mother refused to leave its side, even when prodded by other females of her kind. She stood alone guarding her first offspring from predators as the rest of her herd moved on; a forlorn figure who did not feed, but constantly touched her baby with her trunk, urging it to get on its feet. Some opportunistic scavengers had gathered nearby, a pack of small dog-like creatures and a few enormous vultures, and the mother occasionally made short charges at them to drive them off.

"Such a pitiful scene, but fortunately she is well distracted. This will make a good start to the day," Henri commented in a low voice from where he crouched behind a small clump of low shrubs, forgetting that his current companions could not understand what he was saying. The beaters, including Sinbad and Farhad, had been instructed to stay back for now, and the man who had originally donned the mammoth cape had set it aside as they had no need for further diversion.

The spearmen crept up and gradually surrounded the distressed beast. They had to drop prone several times as a nearby large bull with a broken off tusk tip turned in their direction, but he seemed far too busy pacing around his own herd to bother about some two-legged creatures in the grass near a cow he did not recognize.

Gorriz had been eyeing the bull, and he made a shrill bird call to get everyone's attention. He motioned low for the beaters and Henri's group to come around, and act as a buffer zone between the cow and the next group. The elder hunter was well familiar with the behavior of the animals he stalked. Once the spears began to hit the cow, her trumpets of distress would rise the ire of that too-close male, who was likely already in the aggressive stage of pre-mating season behavior, since they were experiencing the first real thaws of the season. His greatly heightened response to those inner urges might cause that bull to come charging in on these puny competitors who were cutting him off from what was now an abandoned female without a calf.

Even without the male mammoth's intrusion, she would not be easy to bring down. Smaller than the males and younger than most of the breeding age females, she was still very large, and that curving set of tusks on her could do serious damage. They would have to dispatch her quickly and without interference or men could be killed or injured, and there had been too much of that lately. Gorriz was determined not to lose any more hunters, or they would be forced to take young boys and graybeards out with them next time.

That was why he had welcomed these fearless strangers to his party, in spite of how Varg of the Black Fur protested they were interlopers come to steal their women. Even if they were not much help in the actual killing, their assistance freed up men who understood the hunt, so that they could handle spears.

This was a warrior group to be reckoned with in their own lands, that much Gorriz knew by watching them, and yet they had come bearing gifts and asked little in return. His daughter Myeega had spoken reverently of their prowess against the crescent-horned beast. She expounded on how even the small woman traveling with them had been brave and canny, which had earned her the admiration of much of the people, who worshiped the Mother Creator. The strangers had been respectful to Doh Brom, his older sibling, who was clan leader and shamaness. Huyana, the woman who had been chosen to mate with their earth colored leader, proclaimed him an excellent lover and quite gentle, though his hands were calloused from hard work and he bore the muscles of a fighter and the scars of many conflicts. If that mating went well, she might bear his dark skinned child, which would bring good luck to all their people. The giant that traveled with them was certainly impressive, and young Afra was quite taken with the boy.

The thin girl and the small man with the bow he had no opinion of yet, for neither had seemed very impressive, though Doh Brom had insisted that this unmated female be allowed to hunt with the men, and Doh Brom's wishes were always met. The fat male was lazy and unfriendly, but that might be simply because he was a slave.

With everyone in position, Gorriz motioned his hunters forward. They crept stealthily through low brush, snow patches, and winter-flattened tussocks of grass, moving closer to the distressed cow. They could smell her animal reek and the blood of the birth along with the sharpness of fresh dung.

The mammoth's eyes were small and to the sides of their head, making her vision only moderately acute, and far better in a peripheral sense, so that she relied on her sense of smell more. Because of the mess that each hunter had smeared him or herself with, she could not scent them very well, but her hearing was keen, and she was aware of some creatures creeping closer. She raised her head and her ears came forward, and all the men froze, for they were not near enough to throw any spears with accuracy. She remained wary, making a noise that sounded like a low rumbling growl while slinging her trunk back and forth across the calf's body, indicating her willingness to defend him against predators.

The hunting party had spread out, so that a few could attack from either side, while the main body would launch their weapons toward her face and head, the most vital spots. Ralf, with his superior size and strength, had been counted amongst the forward band, and he expected to have to charge in at some point. If she rushed them, these lightly armed men would have no choice but to run off after throwing a spear or two, but the tall Viking had his axe as well, and he welcomed a challenge.

The local people depended on their hunts to eat, and they knew their business. Both flanks attacked first, springing up with spear holders loaded, and sprinting in to throw. The cow mammoth trumpeted and roared as the spears struck her, stumbling forward over her dead calf before turning ponderously to charge the right flank, where Tishimi was late in getting off her shot. Only three of the five spears thrown struck well enough to draw blood, but nothing was in a vital spot.

As the mammoth turned, the hunters facing her came out of a crouch, and raced forward. A hail of five more spears went sailing through the air. Ralf did a little better than he expected with such wobbling shafts, though his throw was high and stuck in the furry hump atop her head. Gorriz's spear vibrated below the left eye, drawing blood, while Varg had hit the base of the trunk right between both eyes. They were still not deep enough in to hit the brain.

The pain-dazed creature screamed and trumpeted in distress, flinging her trunk up to knock or yank the spears free while shaking her head and backing away, as first one side and another of the flanking hunters sent their second spears sailing. More of those hit and stuck around her head and shoulders, and the pain was maddening. She tried to turn and move away, and yet more spears hit her from the forward hunters, making her squeal in agony. With the close proximity of the men around her and the added blood loss, she stumbled back and stepped onto her own dead calf, which made an ugly sound of snapping ribs and squashing innards. Even premature, it weighed almost as much as a full grown man.

They would have taken her down far faster, had not both the nearby bull and the one whose herd she belonged to decided to intervene.

The broken tusk bull was closer, and he stood watching the developing scene with his ears flapping and tail twitching, rumbling a low warning to his nearby cows. Catching an occasional suspicious sight or sound, he took a few decisive steps in the hunting party's direction, swaying his head and slapping his trunk, emitting an occasional drawn out growl. As the men leapt up and began to surround the young cow, throwing their spears, her cries of pain and distress inflamed his mood from natural wariness into infuriated rage. He lifted his trunk and trumpeted once before he came charging in.

For such a large and ungainly looking creature, the mammoth moved very rapidly. The beaters including young Farhad and Sinbad—who had some experience with elephants—raced forward, throwing rocks and clashing spears or blades in the brush, trying to spook and turn him. The archers and slinger came on the run as well, and both stones and arrows pelted the big beast, with Henri's longer-range bow scoring most of the actual hits, though they did not go deep enough through all that coarse hair to cause any serious wounds.

Now under attack himself, the big bull feinted sideways a few times, snorting and tossing his head, ripping at the taller vegetation with his one full tusk. The breeding season was at hand, and all males were edgy, but there was no sense in dying for a single cow when the plains were filling with them.

The broken tusk bull had just about made up his mind to withdraw and go back to the cows he had been traveling with when the bull who had been following the dying cow's herd came charging up behind him. Confronted by small, howling enemies in front flinging stones and stinging missiles, and the far younger prime bull who was scattering all nearby cows in his haste to rush over and gore or flatten whatever was attacking another female, he decided to face the aggressor he understood.

He turned on the other bull, and challenged him.

At first to Sinbad, this seemed like a welcome respite, and so he stopped to catch his breath, but then noted that the beaters around him kept on pursuing the beasts, trying to drive them away. He soon understood why. In their fury, the bulls that were facing off were advancing, backing, and circling with no thought for who or what might get underfoot. Even the other mammoths were moving away to avoid being injured. The spearmen who were fighting to take down the cow were far too busy dealing with her to pay attention to this new threat, and the two angry males were coming very close to where men were running and dodging her gradually weakening but still dangerous feints and charges.

The beaters had run in to join them and help end her struggle, but the two archers were at a loss for what to do to hold back the raging bull mammoths. There weren't enough men to handle both situations. Someone was going to get trampled!

"Ralf, Tishimi, Henri, to me!" Sinbad bellowed, right before he charged the bulls with his scimitar flashing, a thoroughly fired-up Farhad racing at his side.

Sindhi sailors are brave and capable beyond all others, but they are still human. All men of the sea can be superstitious, overlooking the more worldly answers to any crisis. The crew members of the Blue Nymph were no exception and their attempts to outdistance and escape the beasts that were hunting them proved futile. No matter how many backs bent to the oars and how fast they rowed, the pod of killer whales stayed with them. Normal denizens of the ocean did not act that way, so these must be demons disguised as fish.

Sinbad's use of magic had doomed them all, for why else should these creatures attack the ship and be so determined to taste the flesh of mankind; except that her captain and most staunch defenders were all ashore in a mythical land of fire and ice? Were not the seven seas full of fish and other swimming beasts that could be eaten? Perhaps by landing a party of explorers on that accursed shore, it had angered some local god, who raised a horde of protective spirits that took to the water.

Some men prayed against such evil as they plied the oars in vain, and others implored Allah for help as they watched the dawn skies for some sign of a breeze. Becalmed and beset, the ship rocking from the near constant threat of buffeting bodies, with an impenetrable fog both behind and before them, the crewman begged their own god for a miracle.

Omar had even stopped haranguing them, though he still stomped the deck back and forth, bracing himself as the ship rolled and heaved. The most stalwart of those aboard, his mind was focused solely on surviving, not what might have crossed over from the otherworld. There had been a few minor leaks so far, but the Blue Nymph was built well, and the ship's carpenter with Haroun's help had been successful in patching them. The boy was quick enough to bail and haul buckets up to throw the water overboard that it never got past his ankles, though twice the vessel heeled over after a furious blow on one side, and snapping jaws came close to snatching him away. Haroun did not seem overly frightened, for he had been speaking quietly with Rafi, who had told him the nature of such creatures. This left Omar even more disturbed, for now the cabin boy knew more than he did!

After a particularly vicious set of thumps that left yet another small leak, the Blue Nymph's short and burly first mate knew he must swallow his pride and speak with the learned man. He had been reluctant to call for Rafi himself, but if this went on much longer, they would sustain serious damage that might eventually sink them. Even if these creatures were not some kind of ocean-going jinn, they were certainly intelligent enough to take advantage of that situation, and would pick off any man clinging to the wreckage of a sinking ship. There were no other vessels in that netherworld section of sea likely to come to the rescue.

And even if I survived, Sinbad would have my head for losing his beloved Blue Nymph!

"Haroun, fetch me Rafi, I wish to speak with him immediately," Omar shouted over the continuous chanting prayers of the oarsmen and sailors.

The boy scuttled below deck, and came back straightaway with the elder man following right behind him. Haroun glanced uneasily from one to the other, and then he left to go back to his bailing.

"What can I do for you, my friend?" Rafi said quietly with a slight bow. The thin old man almost tipped over sideways as the ship canted drunkenly again, and men whose oars left the water abruptly, called out in fear.

Omar was not one for mincing words. Holding onto a bit of rigging to keep his balance, he snapped, "I am told that you have some understanding of these demonic beasts. Do you know why they attack us?"

Rafi pursed his lips, and similarly braced, he glanced out over the side. "I see no demons here; just the large and dark, fierce dolphins that hunt whales in packs as wolves hunt sheep on land. Since there are no sheep here, nor does there appear to be whales or any other creature of size to feast on, our ship full of warm blooded men must seem like a reasonable substitute."

Omar felt confused. It was true they had not seen any whales nearby, but then not every voyage had shown them. Yet they had never been attacked this way before! "Why would there be nothing for them to feed on? The ocean is vast, and these beasts can swim anywhere!"

It was hard for Rafi to explain something he only barely understood himself. Being buffeted about almost continuously, and hearing the cries of men as they lost footing and nearly went overboard was not helping.

"Omar, did you not notice that that frigid sea before us was fairly shallow water? The moisture that would raise it to normal levels is tied up in those great walls of ice. No large creature can swim well or hunt properly under such conditions, and the cost of keeping a body warm is a belly ever pinched with hunger. These sea wolves are desperate for meat."

"And I suppose we represent that to them," Omar said sourly. "What do you suggest we do now, O' Learned One?" More oars were being savaged, and if that went on much longer, soon they would not be able to make any progress at all.

Rafi stopped for a moment, stroking his beard and thinking hard. "They come very close to the ship, do they not?" At Omar's curt nod, he continued, "Then my suggestion is that we become the hunters instead of the prey. Perhaps we can fashion a spear for killing one of them. I do not know if they will cannibalize their own kind, but with blood in the water, we will at least attract sharks, and that might cause a fight to distract them. If they are hungry enough—and by the way they persist, I suspect they are ravenous—they will eat whatever is easiest to grab."

"That... might... actually work!" Omar said with a half grin. He clapped the thin old man on the back as they turned to make their way back to the hatch. "How did you learn such a thing?"

"I read," Rafi said quietly, carefully keeping the note of triumph out of his voice.

Omar snorted. "I have read the Quran. That is all Allah requires of me!"

Rafi smiled slightly, but it was hidden by his beard. "I too have read the Quran, but I believe that it is good to know many things. Allah is busy; and the man who can help himself does not have to leave every problem to His will alone."

Rafi had moved away before Omar could decide if that was blasphemy or just plain good sense. Another series of thumps and shouts announced that they still were the target of the beasts below.

"Bah, I've no time for debating philosophy! HAROUN!" he bellowed, "Get me that carpenter and tell him to bring his tools!"

He only had a vague idea of how to handle the dangerous situation they were in, but lack of a cohesive plan had never stopped Sinbad before. As he dodged to and fro, trying to keep from being trampled to death, his quick-thinking mind was sizing up the possibilities.

While they posed a significant threat to the any smaller creatures around them, the two mammoth bulls were so locked into their own confrontation, they had forgotten about the besieged cow bellowing behind them, or the puny but effective two-legged predators that were wearing her down. The hunters would not have enough spears left to take out even one of the two male mammoths, and so that would have to be done some other way.

The 'way of the wolf', Henri had called it. Cripple the hindquarters, and the beast would be immobilized and killed far more easily. It was risky, with double the bulk moving heedlessly as the mammoths fought each other, but Sinbad and company had managed it once with the woolly rhino, which had been totally focused on killing them. It could be done again.

He shouted orders in short bursts so as to be heard over the snorting, trumpeting, growling, and shuffling noises the two giant creatures made as trunks locked and slapped, and tusks were used as plows to shove each other around.

"Ralf, we need you to get those legs out from under the broken tusk bull. Farhad, you're with Ralf for now; cover him and assist where you can. Henri, see if you and your new friends can get in a lucky shot to help bring one of them down. Tishimi, you and I are going to have to take the younger bull from behind on our own. Get to work my friends, before someone gets killed!"

The two archers and the youth with the sling followed Henri's gestures for where to set up. The small man from Gaul was good at finding cover, for he seldom liked to fight in the open, and certainly not when there was the chance of being squashed beneath rampaging monsters!

Ralf, having discarded his oversize fur parka, crouched with big bunched muscles standing out beneath his fair skin, ready to rush in as soon as he had an opening. The bulls themselves were so well-distracted by circling and wrestling with one another, they had become oblivious to all but their own rage.

Farhad was a wiry young man on the cusp of manhood, but he had a brash nature and all the courage of youth without the wisdom of years of fighting. He too tossed aside his coat and drew his blade. A middle child of fisher folk, he had only learned some basic moves with it, but he was agile, fast, and clever. He idolized both his adventurous captain and the hulking Viking who had often been friendly to him, and so would do whatever he could to assist them. Thoughts of comely and wanton Afra's reaction to his bravery entered his mind as he set himself up similarly to his sometime mentor, and watched for an opening.

Ralf realized that with the constant back and forth of the struggling beasts he would have to time it just right to cripple a back leg without being crushed beneath it. It had taken many blows to disable the rhino, which had the same sort of long hair and an exceedingly tough hide. He hoped these great elephant-like creatures had less thickness to their pelt, or he was going to have to attack it several times just to get through hair and skin to cut a tendon. That he would be tempting fate twice in such a short period of time, was not lost on him.

Ah well, if he did not survive, there would be a Valkyrie with a horn of mead waiting to greet his spirit and a place set for him at the feasting table in Valhalla. If he lived, those two young widows would be quite warmly welcoming. Either way, a man couldn't lose. Ralf smiled grimly in his frost rimmed beard and squinted in the afternoon sun, awaiting his moment of glory.

The other bull was younger, stronger, and a bit taller. For a while he seemed to have the advantage. He continually pressed forward, trying to head-butt his older opponent backwards onto his haunches so he would be injured, or at least disgraced enough to run off and forfeit his cows. In his swaggering youthfulness, he underestimated the senior bull with the broken tusk, which was the veteran of far more mating season brawls and knew a few tricks. The wily old fellow would give a little ground to put his opponent off guard and then suddenly shift sideways, scooping the other bull's head up with that one good tusk awhile twisting hard with trunk locked around it to pull him off balance. They pushed each other around and struggled together continuously, paring brash temperament and sheer brawn against the guile and cunning craftiness of age and experience. They were making a mucky mess of the entire area, and men were dodging everywhere to avoid those treelike legs and big bumbling feet that could smash an unlucky person flat.

As the younger bull strained and shoved, his hind legs were stretched back to brace him. Tishimi studied him carefully even as she danced out of the way, and she came up with the bold plan. She explained it quickly to Sinbad and he readily agreed, because while they were both skilled and brave, neither of them had Ralf's great brawn, nor did their blades chop as efficiently as his axe. It was impossible to get in more than a swipe or two before they had to back off again.

"You and I must work in stages," she said breathlessly, as they dodged sideways together to avoid being smashed flat as the creatures circled again.

"You and I must work in stages."

"Let me go in first and shave free the hair of this beast—I promise it will not feel the cut. Then you come in and sever the leg muscles." She too had cast aside the bulky fur parka, underneath which she still wore her silk tunic, and only kept the leggings on. Those leggings would not impede her speed that much, but the more heavy coat made it impossible to move as freely with her arms as her technique demanded. Tishimi's dexterity with both keen edged swords depended on being able to dart around rapidly and then dance out of the way. It was something she excelled at, and Sinbad knew that.

"All right, we'll do it your way," he said, similarly tossing off his own parka before lifting again his own deadly curved blade. Sinbad shivered a bit in the frosty air, but he was smiling as well. This was the kind of challenge he lived for. Besides, once they killed these two beasts, there was at least a lucrative load of ivory between them, and the village could have the rest of the carcasses. He had no thoughts of failure, for he had fought through many impossible odds in his lifetime, and had always been victorious.

As the huge creatures sparred yet again, the broken off tusk of the older mammoth snagged and got wedged within the larger part of the curve of one of the younger male's tusks. The beasts pushed and strained inward toward each other, but they remained stuck together and rooted in one spot for a few long moments of trunk slapping, head shaking, and rumbling growls.

Ralf saw his opportunity. He raced in and began hacking away at the long fur mats to get down to the skin beneath. There was a lot of long hair covering the legs and feet of these larger and longer limbed creatures, and because of their size and spread he could only tackle one leg at a time. He had to make sure to get out of the way as the bull shuffled around, trying to free itself. A second attempt and he drew a little blood. The great tail came slapping down as the beast bellowed, splatting coarse and frosty fur tainted with dung into his eyes and mouth, whipping his exposed face raw, and nearly knocking him down. Ralf recovered in time to drunkenly backpedal out of the way, but he had to stop and wipe the mess off his face, spitting out the taste of manure as he did.

"Damn you to Niflheim for that insult; don't I stink enough without having to taste it?"

Farhad rushed in right after him, but all he managed to do was hack off more hair from the opposite back leg before he slipped and fell, and had to roll out of the way to avoid being stepped on. There was no denying that the boy was quick thinking and brave!

Seeing that there was only a small dripping of blood on the leg he'd been worrying away at, Ralf charged right back in and began methodically hacking at it again. He did a small amount of damage in between ducking and running for his life a few more times. He got swatted again with the tail, and decided that was going next.

A furious overhead chop cut the broken tusk bull's tail in half, just hitting the edge of the vertebrae, which also made him squeal and thrash around, jerking the other bull sideways. That put his younger opponent so off balance, he slid and had to brace his back legs to maintain his footing. That moment gave Tishimi her opportunity. She darted in with both swords drawn, and her arms whirled in blurs too hard to follow as she sliced away long mats of hair. She had to dance sideways more than once to avoid being trampled, but both back legs of the beast were well shorn before she retreated.

"Your turn, My Captain," she called out with a slight smile and some gasping in the cold air, as Sinbad pounded past her.

A scimitar is designed as a slashing, chopping blade, and it only has one edge. It is often used on horseback, or in Sinbad's experience for close-in fighting, usually on deck; so it works best in arched and curving downward or sideways strokes. Sinbad had begun working out with a practice sword as soon as he could safely lift it, so to him, his weapon had become an extension of his arm. Since there was no one's blade to block and parry, he charged in swinging. While moving about, he sliced from one angle to the next, in crossing maneuvers that began above his shoulder and hacked downward before he deftly turned the blade and raised it to come back up the opposite way. The undercoat of the beast was thick, and the hide was almost as tough as that of the woolly rhino, but his technique left him on the balls of his feet, so he only had to keep dodging back and sideways to avoid being stepped on or knocked down. Still it took dexterous strength and accuracy as well as quite a few swings to draw any real blood.

Working close-in like that was dangerous, because as the mammoth bull began to feel the sting of the blade over its enraged ardor for besting the older bull it was still entangled with, it began to yank itself sideways to free its locked tusks. After several tries, those two sets of long curving lengths of ivory parted with a resounding scraping noise, and then both beasts were free to turn on and attack their new foes.

Through all the battle of the male woolly mammoths, the archers had not been idle, and they had been able to land a few decent shots. As the bulls finally pulled apart, the older mammoth lost his footing and stumbled backward, nearly sitting down on Ralf. At that moment, while the beast was off balance and unable to move forward, one of Henri's arrows managed to hit an eye, blinding the broken tusk bull on one side. It did not kill the big creature, but seriously slowed it down.

Ralf had somehow managed to scramble out of the way, but lost his blood-stained axe in the confusion. Unfortunately that was now beneath the huge feet of the enraged beast, which was turning rapidly to confront him. The Norseman pulled his knife, and with a maniacal grin, dove back in to grab hold of one rear leg. He dug the blade deep enough to rip through skin in his attempt to sever a tendon he could barely see because of the sudden spray of blood.

The big bull screamed and tossed his head at the first prick, and then kicked backwards, trying to shake his attacker off. Ralf hung on grimly, sawing away with the smaller blade; trying to cripple the leg. Unfortunately he could not let go in time as the huge foot swept back and caught him in the chest. He was thrown hard onto his back, his head hitting a rock, temporarily rendering him senseless.

The limping bull was still upright and he somehow managed to turn. Unable to see well enough to gore the man with his one good tusk, he lifted a huge front foot and made as if to stomp Ralf into the ground. A quick thinking Farhad ran in swinging his own blade, and got in a minor blow, but it drew the mammoth's attention. Off balance, the heavy creature swung its tusks and trunk Farhad's way to sweep him aside, but the broken-ended one could not reach the boy before he could get in another blow. Standing his ground long enough inside that dangerous spot to get in a good cut, Farhad swung his scimitar up over his shoulder as he had been taught by Sinbad, and then put every ounce of strength he had to slash downward, taking off a good chunk of the end of the trunk before ducking back and away, avoiding the following tusk.

Blood gushed and sprayed everywhere as the creature screamed and flailed its severed trunk overhead. No fool, Farhad ran for his life. Henri jogged past him as he retreated, and dropping to one knee, he took careful aim. His shot was perfectly placed, because it went up into that open mouth, clearing the tongue and both sets of the huge, ridged upper teeth, and pierced the soft palate.

The imbedded arrowhead barely nicked the brain, yet coupled with the other wounds it was enough to stop the beast in his tracks. With the combined blood loss from the severed trunk, a pierced eye, and a sliced leg, along with the exhaustion of fighting with a much younger rival, the ponderous creature began to sway and wobble. Its remaining eye glazed over and its legs buckled, as slower than a great forest tree, it collapsed and fell over on the side of the broken tusk, landing with a ground-shaking thud. It twitched a bit as it died and the bloody stump of the trunk as well as the other great tusk wound up draped over a just rising Ralf, doing little additional damage but pinning him to the ground in a shower of gore and mucus.

Some of the native hunters, having finally dispatched the cow, came running over jabbering away in their own language, doing what they could to yank the Viking free. They obviously found it hard to believe that three men, a boy, and a woman had taken down not one, but two prime bulls on their own, without the use of spears. The method that Sinbad and his company had employed was not something they would have thought of, and it made a big impression.

Trying not to wince and be thought of as a weakling, the Norseman struggled to sit up, and then gritted his teeth as he shakily rose to his feet. He ignored the nagging pain in his midsection and the throbbing of his head, and instead blustered over the disgusting condition of his outfit.

"Does every one of these infernal beasts have to smear itself all over me?" he grumbled. He had a mild concussion and perhaps some cracked ribs, but that was nothing that a Viking couldn't walk off. He started searching for his axe, which lay miraculously unbroken beneath one of the great legs of the creature. "Well that's one dead anyway," he said with a wink at a pale faced but similarly grinning Farhad, and then clapped Henri on the back as he strode past.

"That was another good shot," Ralf congratulated him.

"You are not seriously injured?" the little man from Gaul inquired politely as he loped along to keep up with his tall friend's long-legged stride. They were headed over to where Sinbad and Tishimi were contemplating the other bull, who bellowed in defiance, but could not move much on his ruined hind legs.

"Bah, I've had worse injuries fighting with my sisters! Let's see if we can dispatch this one as well," he added, hefting his axe and gazing up at the crippled giant.

"Allow me, my robust friend; you have taken enough of a beating for one day," Henri said as he sighted, drew back as far as his bow would allow, and then let loose. It took two arrows, both well placed in an eye and the base of the trunk between them, but the big beast swayed and finally went down, slumping forward awkwardly, though it was still barely breathing. As an extra measure of caution, Ralf stepped up on one foreleg and chopped open the neck, letting it bleed out to end its feeble final struggles. He wheezed and gasped, trying not to show any pain, but an observant Tishimi noted it and she put a mittened hand on his arm.

"It would be wise to rest now," she said, handing him back his discarded parka. "We have done our part. The women and older men with the cutting tools and hide shelters are here, and they can handle the butchering and skinning. Their people are making fires, and we who have labored hard will soon have hot food and comfort. We have earned that."

"I suppose we have," Ralf rumbled with growing interest and followed the rest of the weary group from the shore party—minus the still absent Saeed—in tramping back toward where conical shelters of hide and stakes from the skids were being raised in a camp around the dead bodies. Embers had been carried in bone cups topped with stones, and after hearths were made, fires were kindled to warm cold bodies and ward off scavenging predators that might be attracted by the smell of blood. Most of the plains beasts had been spooked by the ruckus and the death cries of the three mammoths, and so had moved well away from the trampled area.

With nods and forehead butts from some of the smiling tribe, the hunters and Sinbad's party settled themselves around the nearest fire, and accepted whatever meat was charred enough not to be totally raw. Even Varg came forward to proclaim his admiration, selecting a choice cut of meat and giving it to Sinbad, before stomping off.

It was a crude harpoon at best, but the carefully honed long-bladed knife lashed to the broken oar handle worked well enough for stabbing and slicing. A line had been attached to the far end, so it could be hauled back aboard. Those of the crew who were not involved in rowing or other necessary activities stood around watching the strongest man aboard, a silent loner named Nijad who had chosen to test it, prepare for the ordeal. He lashed himself to the rail, and stood with one foot on the gunwale, the long, smooth shaft in both hands with point downward, waiting as the dull dawn gave way to feeble daylight.

One of the black and white killer whales spotted him and surged upwards, mouth full of sharp teeth opening as it broke the surface. As the head emerged, Nijad thrust the makeshift fishing spear downward with some force, and as Rafi had suggested he caught the beast right between the eye and blowhole. The blade plunged deeply into the creature's flesh before being quickly withdrawn in case another attempt was necessary. With no barbs to hold it in place, it pulled free easily.

The big sea creature bucked and rolled sideways, letting out some sort of long and quavering squeal. That seemed to upset the others, for they all circled around the stricken one as it gasped and squirmed in the water, frantically paddling with one flipper and slapping its tail flukes. It eventually lost its equilibrium and began to slow down as a trickle of blood issued from the still open mouth and air bubbled out through the blowhole. Within a few minutes it rolled on its side and stopped moving.

Its pod mates nudged it and made mewling cries as if in anguish, but the harpooned creature had gasped its last. There were echoing distress calls and a few more half-hearted thumps on the hull of the Blue Nymph, but the big black and white whale killers gradually began to draw away. The men standing around hooted and cheered in relieved appreciation as Nijad raised both hands and held his spear overhead triumphantly. Then Omar sprang to life, issuing orders, and the oarsmen dug in. The Blue Nymph began to come around again and headed away from the rapidly fleeing pod.

Within minutes only the dead body of the beast floated behind them in mute testimony to the savagery of the sea. It already bobbed and heaved as opportunistic sharks gathered to feast on the remains. Rafi watched it quietly as they pulled away, his wrinkled old face with its hooked nose and hawklike gaze not betraying his inner thoughts. He did not even question why Omar and the other crew members had not come forth to congratulate him on this grand idea that had gotten them out of serious danger. It was enough that it had worked. He wondered though at the reaction of the rest of the killer whales in trying to help their injured member, and not taking advantage of its death to slake their hunger.

Nothing in nature is ever wasted, and each life taken fed another life; and yet, these simple-minded, soulless beasts had ignored a free meal and left their deceased brethren behind, consecrated to the sea like a dead sailor. Could it be that they had some rudimentary intelligence and emotions? It was a puzzle that would occupy his astute mind for the rest of the journey.

Evening's darkness still fell fast at that time of year. Even with most of the village adults turned out to help with the butchering, it went slowly, for with the immense size of a mammoth, only the upper side of any carcass could be reached. The cow was tackled first, as her flesh was considered tenderer and less gamey. The calf was mostly spoiled from being squashed, though a few choice pieces were carved free. Only the best bits were taken from the bulls, for a feast in celebration of the great hunt. Any bones that were loosened were tossed on the fire, and while the clinging meat and fat sizzled and charred, letting out a stink, they gave good heat and light, sparing the precious supply of kindling wood.

Hides that could be reached were flayed off to be rolled and bundled with sinew cordage. They would be hauled back to the village to be scraped and cured. Any meat that could not be eaten that night was stacked in big chunks covered with old hides and situated between fires to keep it from being stolen by predators. That also would be packed out the next day. The feet, trunks, jowls, and fat from head and shoulder humps seemed to be considered prized delicacies. The butchering left pools of blood, offal, and rank gore on the ground that normally would have attracted flies, had the weather not turned cold again. The chill wind off the plains swept some of the stench away.

A loose pack of a lighter weight breed of wolf than the ones Sinbad's party had seen chasing the giant deer surrounded the butchering camp, their yellow eyes shining in the flickering firelight. The people chased them off when they got too close or became snappish, but the wolves helped warn of larger predators, so they were allowed to strip those parts of the carcasses that would not be needed or desired. The season of plenty was now upon them all. Dog-like snarls and growling could be heard all around the camp. Now and then someone tossed away a bone or a gristly bit, and one of the braver of the canines would slink forward long enough to grab it before dodging away again into the darkness.

Whatever could not be saved, along with the big bones of the three creatures, would be left in place for now. Once free of meat and gore and dried by the wind and weather, the skeleton would be sectioned and collected for building material and fuel for fires. Contrary to usual practice, all tusks that could be reached had been chopped free, to be presented to the guests in thankfulness for their assistance. Each of the great curving spans seemed to weigh well over one hundred pounds, and the lengthiest pair were longer than their boat!

Sinbad and his company had originally wanted to leave the next day, but he sat tired and puzzled that evening, staring at those huge and heavy lengths of valuable ivory, wondering how he was going to get it all back to the Blue Nymph.

"Much of that meat will spoil," Henri observed as he plucked strands of it from his teeth. "That is why they are picking the best to eat now, and selecting the next best to be dried and smoked for later. Although with meat as tough and stringy as this, I wonder why they bother. There is much game out there," he swept a hand out to indicate the plains around them, "that would be far more palatable."

Sinbad nodded, but his mind was elsewhere. "I am sure they know their business. I am more concerned right now on how we will get our share of this hunt back to the ship."

"We could section them and then build a raft to haul it along behind the boat," Ralf suggested between bites. He had been gnawing on a slice of bloody rare roast haunch lopped off with his knife and caught in one big hand while it was being turned on a makeshift spit. It was tough, gamey, and chewy, but the Viking had eaten worse, and he was ravenous. Sinbad had nibbled a bit and found that the taste did not agree with him, though he ate dutifully so as not to insult their hosts. Tishimi satisfied her hunger with the smallest morsels she could consume to ease the pinched emptiness of her stomach.

"I did not see much wood here," Sinbad replied unhappily. There was little in the way of trees, most of the hard stemmed plants being small shrubs bent crooked by heavy winter snows and cold plains winds.

"No," Ralf said with some hesitation, "But we'll find something. They have wooden spears, and the stakes for their tents and drags are made of wood. There has to be some place around here that they get it from."

"If only we could speak with them!" Henri complained, and the other two men nodded. The lack of a common language was a constant problem.

Tishimi had been quiet up until then, watching the temporary camp bustling around them and the small gathering of predators just beyond. She turned toward Sinbad and said, "These people seem knowledgeable of everything but the sea. Yet this peninsula is hemmed in by ice and so it is like an island, though their ancestors had to get here somehow. If they have wood, they will know where it is. I will ask Doh Brom when we get back to the village."

"How will you do that?" Henri asked curiously. "They barely do more than grunt." His day with the archers and the boy with the sling had been long and frustrating, for everything had to be indicated by gestures.

"We talk in pictures, drawn in sand," Tishimi related. Henri snorted, and she turned to glare balefully at him, her eyes narrowed. "These are intelligent people, and while they do have their primitive ways, they are not savages. You would do well to respect them; you might learn something."

Before Henri could retort, they were interrupted by a series of subdued howls, followed by deep, low toned roars and lengthy growls punctuated by snarls and some sort of ruckus. It all came from the direction of the larger of the two fallen bulls, and everyone on the campsite was instantly alert. Whatever it was had come much too close. Several men grabbed the few spears they had left and with a couple of makeshift torches fashioned of resinous pine scrub wrapped with plaited woven grass, they set off to scare away this latest interloper.

"I suppose we should join them," Sinbad said, rising wearily to his feet. Ralf was already up, chewing the last mouthful of the tough meat while reaching for his axe. Farhad was off somewhere with Afra, but Tishimi and Henri got up as well. Sinbad looked at them and shook his head curtly. "I appreciate your loyalty my friends, but it is pitch black out there. We have no idea what we are facing, and you are both lightly armed. Stay here for now, and if it sounds like we need assistance, grab a spear or club and come join the battle."

Tishimi remained on her feet, and Sinbad gave her a look. "That was an order, by the way," he added sternly before turning to go off.

She dropped gracefully back into a cross-legged position, and practiced her breathing techniques to master her anger.

"You are upset with him," Henri observed as he sorted through his remaining arrows, checking to see which of the recovered shafts would still be usable.

"I do not understand why men think all women are helpless. I have faced many dangers with and without Sinbad, and at no time was I ever a liability. He treats me as a child."

Henri sympathized with her frustration, even though he was perfectly content to drowse by the fire and let others handle the current situation. He, too at times longed for the respect he felt he was owed. Still, Sinbad was right: without sufficient light and equipped with only modest weapons, they would only get in the way. Besides, the experienced hunter knew just by the sound of the creature what it was they were facing. The bow would not do him much good at night, and neither would Tishimi's lightweight if exceedingly sharp swords. They were fine for close-in fighting, but not proof against brutes with long claws and a mouth full of sharp fangs. He tipped his head in the direction of the commotion. Loud echoing growls and savage snarls were joined by the shouts of men.

"That is a bear out there, and from the sound of it, a very large and hungry one. I too wish to assist where I may, but a bow is at a disadvantage in the darkness, and I am not trained in blades or spears. It is not easy to be a man, and be left behind while the bigger, bolder ones gain all the glory."

She nodded, and pulled from her pouch a sharpening stone she used in deft strokes to hone her already keen-edged blades. Her head down, Tishimi concentrated on dressing the metal, the soothing rhythm of whetting easing her troubled mind.

"I do not look for accolades. I fight where I believe I am needed, and only for the good of all," she explained after a few moments of silence. "I desire to be respected as a warrior, not coddled for being a woman."

Henri was about to say something candid and comforting, when the racket of the fight with the bear came closer—a lot closer!

"You may get your wish yet, for it is coming this way!" he shouted, leaping to his feet with bow already strung and arrow nocked.

Even in the eerie flickering of the torches, it was soon evident what was going on. A huge brown bear bruin, newly awakened from winter hibernation and exceedingly hungry, had arrived; and he was warning the wolves away from scavenging the kill. The smell of blood and death had drawn him, and after circling the camp in the darkness, he had chosen the kill farthest from the firelight. While these big bears were often scavengers, they had a reputation for being bullies when it came to robbing meat caches. To secure his claim he had already injured several wolves, and killed one with a huge sweep of his heavily clawed front paws.

By the time Sinbad and Ralf had arrived, the wolves had backed off and the men with their light throwing spears had started making feints at the bear. It seemed they were not as interested in killing it as driving it away, but the creature had no such clemency for its annoying two-legged attackers. An elder man had not moved out of the way fast enough when it charged, and he lay twitching and bleeding out from a savaging by those big canine teeth, with a lacerated scalp and arms, and face half ripped off. Another man had been swatted away with a long clawed forepaw, and he

"The bear is coming this way!"

groaned with a shoulder and arm torn open. The rest of the men were wary, but determined that this creature would leave if they harried it enough.

"Why do they not kill it?" Sinbad snapped in frustration as he attended to the wounds of the grateful hunter that Ralf had dragged out of harm's way. The two outsiders had been strictly ordered back, while the experienced men dealt with the situation.

"I suspect that it has something to do with a clan belief," Ralf said with obvious disappointment as he leaned on his axe. "Did you notice how their witch woman was dressed? She wore bear furs, teeth, and claws. Perhaps the bear is one of their god symbols."

"Well their god is about to join them for dinner!" Sinbad said with alarm as the bear broke through the ranks of spear holding men, knocking someone over in the process, before turning and bounding away into the interior of the camp.

Tishimi was up and armed, ready to face yet another nightmare creature. What came hurtling in was a huge bear with shaggy brown fur, three inch claws, and huge canine teeth. It was pursued by men with spears and torches trying to herd it away, as well as Sinbad and Ralf with their own weapons. Initially the big creature was flat out on all fours, but it stopped and growled when more people from the settlement came forward with whatever weapons they could find, with the intention of getting it to back off and leave. Still quite groggy and out of sorts from hibernation, the bear had decided to run rather than stand its ground against so many aggressors, but now was caught at bay between the ones behind, the ones in front, and the fires.

With a long and hollow-sounding roar it turned back into the shadows between two of the conical tents, but got tangled in the lashings that held one of the structures to stakes in the ground. In its struggle to be free, the frantic creature tore part of the covering down. There were screams from inside as the structure collapsed sideways, for two women and a few children had huddled there in fear.

Not very stable in the thawing ground, some of the poles keeping the tent upright pulled loose and came crashing down onto the bear itself. Already over stimulated, the angry and confused beast went up on two legs to defend itself against this new enemy. Towering almost ten feet over all, it began swiping long clawed front paws out, knocking even more of the structure over.

Henri was moving around, trying to get a clear shot, when Farhad came racing past with a native spear in hand. His intention was to show off for Afra, but he did not understand the use of the specialized weapon. This was not a heavy shafted fighting spear or pike to hold onto and jab with, but a lightweight throwing javelin for tossing from a distance. He got too close, and one swipe of a big paw knocked the spear from his grip and spun him around, ripping through his clothing and laying open long bloody slashes on his upper arm, back, and shoulder. If not for the fur parka, and his smaller size than the grown men offering less resistance against the blows, those claws would have peeled the flesh from him.

Afra screamed as blood darkened his furs, and she ran to help Farhad. The bear went down on all fours again and lunged in their direction, but stopped when Tishimi leapt before it, flashing her blades in a whirlwind of action. The sheer energy of her movements were mesmerizing, and her ever-spinning swords seemed to throw sparks that dazzled in the firelight. The bear backed off uncertainly, for those gleaming lengths of steel resembled all too much the lightning that arced down from the sky and kindled the wildfires that scorched and killed. Without any thought for herself, the small but determined Oriental woman continued her sword dance, driving the nine foot long, eight hundred pound bruin backwards.

Henri wove through the chaos trying to find the right angle, but it was dangerous to shoot with Tishimi in the way and all the people milling around watching her in awe. Just as the archer from Gaul got lined up for a decent shot, Sinbad came up and put a restraining hand on his arm.

"Don't do it my friend; these people seem to revere the creature. Let it go."

As if it understood, the bear—snapping and snarling—made a final half-hearted rush at the camp defenders before turning to lope away into the night.

"That is ridiculous!" Henri snapped as he lowered his arms, for he had seen the bodies brought in. "It tore into two of them, and injured young Farhad, and yet they will let it escape?"

"It is their way," Sinbad said quietly. Afra and an elder woman were looking over Farhad's wounds, which were superficial, though they would likely give him a few scars. The boy was sitting up and sipping something from a bone cup. The wounded hunter had also been given a draught—presumably for his pain. A hysterical middle-aged daughter was rocking, sobbing, and wailing over the death of her elderly father, whose mangled head lay in her lap.

Tishimi dropped her arms so that her swords hung point down, and exhaled. The danger was over. She had driven the great creature away. She did not hear the noise of the camp behind her, or the appreciative cheering of the people who had witnessed her impromptu solo performance. She turned and walked resolutely back toward the fires to the chant of, "Doh Brom Tuh-Shee-Mee! Tuh-Shee-Mee Grav! Tuh-Shee-Mee Bai Coor!" She did not understand all the words, but the meaning was evident. All the men—including the lead hunter Gorriz and Varg of the Black Fur—bowed their heads and proclaimed her to be a warrior both brave and wise. The women gave a tremolo call in appreciation, and several ran to fetch her hot broth and special little food delicacies. Tishimi just sat quietly alone and stared into the fire, until her male companions rejoined her.

No one broke the silence until Sinbad himself spoke. Always the astute leader, he had caught the tone of respect given Tishimi by the men of the village, and felt her companions owed her some recognition of their own.

"That was incredibly courageous, and you likely saved both Farhad and Afra's lives, as well as those of the innocent members of this group who would have been tempting fate to drive that beast away. Sometimes I believe we forget that not only are you are one of us, but you have skills and knowledge of your own to complement ours. Men think of courage in terms of strength of muscle and prowess with weapons, but women... Women have the courage of lionesses to protect their own, and that belies their less powerful bodies. Women also have the gift of wisdom, which makes them unafraid to try other ways of doing things. You have been an asset to my company from the day you signed aboard."

"Here, here," Ralf said, raising his own bone cup of broth in a toast, and wishing it was ale.

Henri winked at Tishimi, and added, "Yes and since most of the fair sex are not hard on the eyes either; so we have the best of all worlds."

Tishimi glanced quickly around at her friends with wary and somewhat disbelieving eyes, but her lips bore the slightest of smiles. They were quite a study in contrasts, yet there was no mistaking that these were all men amongst men. It took her a few moments to compose herself, in which she stared deeply into the fire, thinking about how mankind needed its warmth and light as well as its ability to stave off the unknown things prowling around just beyond their ability to sense. When she spoke, it was in a voice that was low, and thoughtful.

"I am humbled by this praise, but I only did what I knew must be done, as any warrior would. Here, it has been accepted that I can be an equal amongst men, but many other places, I have needed to prove my ability. I am neither weak nor incapable, nor do I feel unusual in any way, just because I am a woman bearing weapons. I do not expect to be lauded for taking this path in life, for it is the only one before me. So please; no more of this special treatment." She looked up and glanced around at her companions sidelong, before continuing.

"I feel I must remark though, after seeing how foolish Farhad almost got himself killed, that if most men thought harder with the brain in their head than with those lower parts that often make their worst decisions, more of you would survive into your dotage!"

"Where's the fun in that?" Ralf quipped, thinking fondly back on his sleeping partners of the past evening. Henri and Sinbad both laughed, and even Tishimi's eyes crinkled in amusement.

They would never change, these men, and perhaps that was how it should be.

They wound up spending yet another day traveling back and forth to the village, helping to haul meat and hides. The pole drags with their rough leather slings—Henri referred to them as travois—proved invaluable, as even women could haul fairly heavy loads on them. Grooves were worn in the ground from many generations of packing out meat and bone this way. Sinbad and Ralf both took their turns at manning them and pronounced it the easiest way to bring along a heavy weight in record time. By dark fall, all the meat that could be harvested, along with the green hides, had been brought back to the camp. To celebrate, there was another hot soak, a late feast, and night of far much more tame debauchery, because everyone was exhausted.

"Captain Sinbad, I wish to speak with you," Farhad called out that evening as they all headed toward their respective sleeping places, and Sinbad paused to let the very sore and tired young man limp over to where they could speak privately. He had a feeling he knew what was coming. Farhad was in some pain, but not so much that he did not do his share of the work, nor would he miss sleeping in the furs of ever-present Afra, who attended his every need. Farhad had motioned her off when he stepped forward to speak with his superior, and she went into her own dwelling to await him.

"You want to take her with us," Sinbad said quietly, as the young man drew himself up and tried to find the words that he was reluctant to speak.

"No, that would not be fair to Afra. This is her life; it is all she has ever known. She could not travel aboard with me, and she would have no family or friends in any port where I would have to leave her whenever we were away. I will not return to fishing for a living just to be home at the end of a day. Besides, this land... it captivates me!" His eyes sparkled, whether it was from the herbal brew they had given him for pain, or his own reckless youth and enthusiasm. "I wish to stay here."

Sinbad was taken aback, but covering his surprise, he looked down at the boy with a mixture of stern mentor and fatherly concern. Was Farhad already that much in love with the native girl that he would forfeit his opportunity at seeing the world and gaining wealth beyond imagination?

"Farhad, I am not sure you have thought this out properly. We have only been here a couple of days, and you might in time grow disenchanted with this life. If we leave without you, there is no way you can reach us if you change your mind, and no guarantee we will ever be able to come back. You will be alone amongst strangers in a place that is bitterly cold and uncivilized, filled with hard labor, dangerous beasts, and the specter of starvation in lean seasons. You will never again feel the warm tropical sun or the kiss of the salt spray. The waves will not rock you to sleep when the moon rises. Think well on that tonight, and then talk to me in the morning, for it is then we are leaving."

"I will," Farhad promised, "but my mind will not change," he added as they went their separate ways. He had already chosen his desire for the slender young woman who warmed their furs as the one thing he could not live without. Sinbad would never understand that, for no female but the Blue Nymph captivated him. His life's joy was on the rolling ocean waves, headed to the next adventure.

In the morning, he had his answer, as the boy who was now a man said his solemn goodbyes, and then went to sit with the village's grizzled flint knapper, watching and learning his new trade. Afra beamed at him with love and happiness from where she worked amongst the women, cutting strips of meat to dry. The people of the village seemed to accept him as one of them.

So be it was that young Farhad was to be left behind when they began their journey back toward the rocky shore. His share of any coin from this voyage would be given to his family. If they ever came back, and he lived to see it, perhaps he could be an intermediary between the village and the Blue Nymph. Sinbad would love to have a full cargo of ivory some day.

After their cooperative collaboration on moving the spoils of the hunt, Sinbad felt secure in having Tishimi ask for assistance in getting their own prizes back to where they had left the boat. Doh Brom had agreed to lend enough men to get the tusks cut up and bundled onto several travois that she donated to them. There was an alder swamp a day's trek south where the people could get more of the abundant wood, and they had plenty of hides to spare. Dried sinew was in smaller supply, but eked out with rawhide and bark fiber, they would have enough cordage to carry their bundled loads of ivory lengths lashed in firmly.

Early morning of their third day in that icy land, they stood back on the ridge above the village, saying their goodbyes to the principal members of the group before donning the grass and mammoth wool padded leather straps that would allow them to move the travois all day. Even Doh Brom had hiked up to bless their journey, and she had loaned them two men to help drag the ivory back to the bluff above the shore. From there they would have to pack it down themselves, for the villagers would go no further. Another kind of people had made the trail down, was all Tishimi could tell them, and Doh Brom's clan had some kind of prohibition about crossing into their territory. In fact, the strange flat headed skull on Doh Brom's staff had belonged to one of them, killed in battle by an ancestor.

Henri heard that explanation and his thoughts went back to the strange-gaited party with the heavy spears that he had seen at a distance when they were descending the ridge toward the plains of hunting. He would be especially vigilant in case of an encounter along the way, so his mind was occupied with scouting ahead. Since the party had extra help, Tishimi and Henri were able to walk freely, carrying only their own belongings and weapons. They were the lookouts, before and behind.

Henri took the forefront, for of them all he was the best at tracking and trail blazing, and he had the sharpest eyes. Behind him came Ralf harnessed to his own travois and dragging it like a plodding ox. He did not complain about the pain in his chest or the shortness of breath. The memory of the widowed sisters' cool little hands wrapping thin sheets of wet hide to bind his ribs when it dried made him smile through the discomfort. Next came Sinbad similarly burdened, with the two village men bringing up the rear. Sinbad also sounded winded, for to spare Ralf, he had insisted on taking the heaviest load for himself. The two village men pulled their own loads without any complaint, for this was the kind of work they did almost daily to survive.

Tishimi brought up the rear, her senses acutely alert for any potential problems. The plains below when viewed through the scrub were filled with great creatures, and now and then something climbed the ridge nearby. Since none of them were bears, she touched her neck and smiled. She had been gifted with one of Doh Brom's necklaces of bear teeth and claws, which she supposed was a ward against further encounters. Since Tishimi did understand such things, she prized it highly, and thought much of the elder warrior woman who had befriended her as a kindred spirit. Doh Brom had seen to it she was outfitted with a few essential items for traveling, including a wooden pot of herb scented grease for cold, cracking skin.

The cause of the visible grooving of the path they had walked in on was now apparent, as dragging lengths of numerous travois over many generations had worn it in the soil. The poles were spaced to take advantage of that, and the way had been gradually cleared of rocks and any brush that might impede their passage. Surprisingly the spread of weight over the long poles fitting into those grooves made the loads feel far lighter, and so they made good time. It was approaching midday as they came to the area where the wooly rhinoceros had been killed. Henri was taking his new responsibility as scout and guide quite seriously, and for once it was easy to see why Sinbad had picked him up as a companion. This was the sort of thing the little archer from Gaul excelled at.

Henri's sharp eyes spotted several things amiss on the slope below, and he abruptly called a halt. "What is it?" Sinbad called to him impatiently.

"Take a short rest, for I see something that concerns me. I will be back in a few minutes," he answered quietly. He was soon lost amongst the boulders and scrub, for being a small man and a hunter by trade, Henri could move like a stalking cat when he wanted to.

Everyone had some sips of water and dried meat. Before they were done, Henri was back up the trail to them, and his look was grim. He held a blood-stained scimitar.

"Saeed," Sinbad said, after a cursory examination. He looked up from the blade to Henri. "His body lies below?"

The small man nodded. "There is little left to identify him as human," he said quietly. "Just some blood-stained cloth, scattered bones nearly picked clean, and this." He pointed to the blade. "As far as I can tell, he was attacked by some large creature while trying to shave meat off that carcass. Most of what is left has gone to the wolves and bears, but it was something else that killed him—a beast with great slashing claws or teeth. He never had time to draw his blade. His remains are spread over a wide area, mingled with the leavings of the hairy beast we fought and animal dung from those who feasted on them both. I have no idea what happened to his skull. This was all I could bring back that was recognizable."

"Then we shall lay that to rest at sea in his memory, once we are under way. For now, I want to get to those bluffs over the beach before dusk, so that we can let these men leave, before they lose the light. There will be a moon tonight, and we can use that light to haul these loads down to the beach. Tomorrow we will put back out to sea as soon as we figure out a way to convey all this ivory back to the Blue Nymph."

"I have some ideas on that," Henri said as he helped lash Saeed's sword to one of the travois. They were back on their way within minutes, and Sinbad ordered that they pick up the pace to make up for the time lost.

They were approaching the area where they had first ascended to the ridge, when the village men indicated they would go no further. Sinbad had no choice but to let them leave. The bluffs over the coast were still well ahead, and the path before them was not as well trimmed or defined.

"I have no idea how we will get these two extra loads down there," he said unhappily.

"If we make it to the cliff edge, we might be able to just toss everything over," Ralf suggested.

"No, ivory is fragile," Sinbad said. "We've already had to cut it up in order to haul it. I don't want it all checked and cracked too."

Ralf frowned, and crossed his arms over his sore chest. "Well, we're going to lose the sun soon. Maybe we should just leave it here for tonight, and plan on camping on the beach. We can make some shelters from the poles and hide."

"With no fire, it will be a cold night," Sinbad cautioned. "We cannot afford to burn these sticks if we are to make a raft."

"I don't have any better ideas," Ralf countered.

"As I recall," Henri broke in, "There were caves nearby. Perhaps we should leave our travois loaded for now, and head down to find a shelter in a warmer spot. Then we can rest in some comfort for the night, and figure out a way to haul our burdens down tomorrow."

"It's about as good a plan as any," Ralf said with a shrug, and they all agreed.

They dragged the travois as close up to the edge of the cliff as possible.

Sinbad unfastened Saeed's blade, and tucked it into his sash before refastening his parka. "I do not think we should tempt fate and leave a potential weapon behind us," he explained. "Now let us be on our way."

With the sun setting behind them, they made their way down the narrow pathway to the beach below. The last third of the trek was made in deepening dusk. While they were discussing what to do, Tishimi had thoughtfully cut a few long lateral branches of aromatic pine scrub and wound them with plant stems rubbed with the scented grease to use as torches. They would burn only fitfully, providing they could find a way to light them. Henri or Ralf would have that skill.

Thankfully their boat was still drawn up on the beach, untouched. It was hard to tell in the growing dusk with the fog rolling in, but it did not seem as if the Blue Nymph was anchored nearby. With the amount of ice bobbing offshore, perhaps Omar had decided to move it to deeper water. They would look again in the morning. The issue now was to find shelter for the night.

"Let us find one of those caves you spoke of, Henri," Sinbad insisted as they trooped farther up the beach. "And quickly, before we lose the light. I dread spending a night out here in the open." At least the wind off the glaciers did not howl down at that lower level, though it was still bitterly cold at night.

All along that rugged and receded shoreline there were the pockmark openings of what were once sea caves, carved by waves laden with sand and silt into the chalky limestone base of the bluffs. Now well above the tide because of the recession of the oceanfront due to the glaciers tying up precious moisture, they offered at least a chance at shelter. Many were too far up the side of the bluff to reach, but a few nearby, where the crescent of shoreline curved inward, were down at an accessible level.

The first cave they found showed signs of having a small spring leaking into it from cracks above, which would make it clammy and uncomfortable. They took some drinks and refilled their water skins from the clear source, and moved on. The next one was all but impossible to approach because of the steepness of the crumbling rock, and the sunset casting shadows on their side of the bluff made dangerous climbing rather dubious. The third one had but a small bit of floor before it dropped off into a crevasse, but there was a cave below and to the left that had a brush covered opening just wide enough for one person to slip into at a time. It was, strangely enough, a bit brighter in there as well. The air in the opening was fairly fresh, and it felt cool, but not cold.

"This is likely a lot bigger inside than the opening suggests," said Sinbad, who in his travels had the most experience with caves. "There is air coming out, so there should be no gasses to steal our breath or explode if we light a fire. I would prefer to scout the interior first, but we have run out of daylight, so this must do."

Darkness was almost upon them, and Sinbad ordered that torches be lit. Ralf set to working on one with his strikers and a pinch of char cloth, while Tishimi and Henri scouted for driftwood, brush, or whatever they could find that would burn. It would not be much of a fire, but well nursed, it would help moderate the chill and keep predators away.

"Let me go first, for we must be certain that it is unoccupied," Sinbad insisted. "I will not risk any of you for that." Grabbing one of the lit torches he thrust it ahead of him and then slipped into the dark opening.

"It's big, and relatively dry. Come in," he called back to them, his voice echoing hollowly in the cavern, and the mixture of relief and enthusiasm in it buoyed their spirits.

Henri and Tishimi soon followed: their unoccupied arms full of whatever wood they could carry. Only Ralf had a tough time getting in, for he was both too tall, and too wide. He had to enter sideways and partially crouched down, and just managed to squeeze through, which aggravated his rib pain.

"Why does every place we stay have to be designed for underfed dwarves?" he grumbled.

"Perhaps your mother should not have hired a giantess to be your wet nurse," Henri countered. "Too much of a good thing, eh?"

"Perhaps yours should not have dropped you on your head, assuring that you didn't grow any taller or wiser than a swaddling," Ralf countered as he used his axe to break up some of the bits of wood they had gathered for kindling.

"It is not the height of a man that matters, but what courage lies inside of him," Sinbad commented as he set aside Saeed's sword so that he and Tishimi could look around carefully. The floor was sand and rock, and there were a few bones, but all seemed to be animal and old, with no signs of human occupation. He was acutely mindful of what Doh Brom's people had said about there being others in the area who were not friendly.

"You see? Even our captain understands my worthiness to this expedition," Henri countered with a self-satisfied smirk as he shaved kindling and Ralf created the spark to light it. "Great height is not always a benefit, for I can go places you cannot. It is also not the dimension which matters most to the ladies," he added with a wink before leaning forward to breathe little puffs of air on the tiny embers that started a single flame glowing. There was a draft that started at the opening they had come into, and it pulled smoke away from the fire toward the back of the cavern, so he made use of that. He sat up and fed the small blaze bits of tinder until it caught, and then glanced up at Ralf with a raised eyebrow. "I always say, nature compensates a man for what he lacks. Therefore, though I may be short, not all of me is so small."

"Your conceit certainly isn't puny," Ralf countered as he hunkered down next to the fire to watch what little of the starlit sky and lapping water he could see through the cave opening. He held out one hand, turning it from back to front, studying it as if never having seen it before. "Your ideas are a bit off too. The gods make a true man well-proportioned. For instance, I have large hands and large feet, so you know the rest has to follow the same pattern."

They would have gone on that way for a while, had Sinbad not called out excitedly from somewhere in the darker recesses in back of the cave, "I cannot believe our fortune! This place is a treasure trove!"

Daylight brightened the gloom, though the fog surrounding the Blue Nymph didn't lift. It was just light enough for the crew to realize that they had drifted far off course. The wind was fitful at best, and never seemed to come from the same direction. There was no sight of any land, and with the sky veiled in overcast, nothing but a dim glow of the sun's ball could just barely be made out.

Omar had taken out the astrolabe and charts designed by the celebrated Persian father and son Al-Fazari, who were notable mathematicians. Their work was impeccable, and had always been of great use to him, yet now it helped not at all. Nothing seemed to line up the way it should by his own reckoning, and he grumbled to himself about it.

He had no idea how to get back to where they had left Sinbad, nor could he seem to find the warmer seas they had sailed in from. While Omar did not fear a mutiny under normal circumstances, once the men knew they were lost, they would begin to panic. Alarmed and distressed men did not follow orders well. He was their leader aboard with the captain ashore, but unlike Sinbad, Omar did not captivate followers with his charisma;

he was used to blustering and swinging his cane to get men's minds back on business. That only worked as long as the majority believed him to be firmly in charge. If hysteria began to take over where practical minds should be focused, he would soon lose control of the crew, and then they would make the decisions, not he. That might very well wind up being a unanimous call to leave Sinbad and his company behind in order to save themselves, and one man did not stand much of a chance as the voice of dissent.

He did not hesitate this time in calling for Rafi. The burly little first mate was very blunt and more open with his concerns than Rafi had ever seen him. They spoke low and well away from anyone who might overhear what was said.

"We are seriously off-course, and may well be lost. This cursed fog has trapped us like my fourth wife did, taunting with veils that hide its treacherous nature. All I can say for sure is that we have left behind the waters I know, and I cannot seem to navigate us back to where we came in. Nothing here matches the design of the world!"

Rafi nodded sagely and looked at the charts and the astrolabe, and then up at the sky. The sun was in the wrong position for morning. As strange as it seemed, they had somehow gotten behind it. He had studied a set of ancient mystical scrolls once, which spoke of such a thing, though he did not understand it at the time.

"I believe," the learned elder man said slowly, so that Omar could grasp the concept, "that this has to do with the magic of the etheric devices. I have suspected since the frozen land came into sight that we have gone somewhere back in time, and this confirms that theory for me. I have read that the past stretches out behind our time like a well-traveled path, though it is usually so obscured by the attractions of the present, we never see this vast world of yesterday outside of our dreams. Knowing this, I would say we are in a netherworld area somewhere between where we came from, and where we left Sinbad."

Omar could barely wrap his mind around such an esoteric idea. He was a man of actions and deeds, not one of speculative concepts beyond his simple faith in his god and his own abilities.

"Bah—that sounds like nonsense! Still, we must get out of here, or this crew will whisper against me, and there will be trouble. What must I do?"

Rafi also was concerned about the attitude of the common sailors, for the safety of the ship depended on them.

"I do not think regular navigation will work here. Perhaps we cannot

They spoke low and well away from anyone who might overhear...

find that land again until we repeat the process which got us there in the first place. As I recall, the Norseman Ralf had chanted a song of his frosty homeland, and then the vision appeared. Is that not so?"

Still bent over his charts, Omar looked up and grimaced. "That is what they claimed, though why that giant's voice would open the way is beyond me. I have heard sick camels that could hold a better tune."

Rafi suppressed a smile. Ralf's voice was deep and grating, so he did not sing often. Haroun was another matter; the boy was always making some noise, and he picked up tunes rather quickly.

Something about that tickled the old man's mind. Omar was blustering again, and Rafi waved him to silence. "Please my volatile friend, allow a man to think in peace," he begged, holding his bony hands atop his topi, as if his head would explode. "I have an idea that wants to be born. Just give me a few moments to grasp it."

"Fine," Omar said gruffly as he began to stomp away. He stopped and turned, and added, "but come up with something soon, or I will have an insurrection to deal with."

Ralf and Henri came running to see what the commotion was about. Tishimi had already seen what lay ahead, and so she stepped back to let them peer in. Sinbad was almost beside himself with glee, for he was the one who had discovered the cache, by following the thin trail of smoke from the fire.

There in the back of the cavern they had chosen for the night, was a yet another opening, and this one was far larger, though it twisted in curves. A few steps inside, and the smell of old death and fresher, colder air permeated the area. Sinbad's crude torch did not throw much light, but it was enough to show him that it led into a chasm beneath a sinkhole a good eighty feet atop the plains. At the base of it lay thick layers of skeletons and partially mummified long dead bodies from many creatures, with a healthy portion of them being mammoths. There were tusks throughout the mess, many of which were either broken or at least separated from the rest of the remains, as more silt and bodies had fallen in to crush what lay below. Most plains creatures were represented, including the woolly rhinos, bison with thick and curving horns, both the large and a smaller sort of deer, a giant breed of cattle that was known as Aurochs, and several kinds of predators. It was a jumbled mess, but Sinbad knew even with a day's work, they could tease out several hundred pounds more of ivory. In two days with more men, he'd have a hold filled. Since it was not completely exposed to weathering, most of it was in good to excellent shape, and would command a very handsome price.

"We are going to be very, very wealthy if we can find a way to transport most of this back with us," the overjoyed captain said. "For tonight, we must rest, because tomorrow we will see what we can do about getting our other load down here, and then perhaps drag some of this largesse out."

Fortunately there were also many dry bones to burn, which would keep them warm that night. While Tishimi guided them with torches and Henri tended the fire, Sinbad and Ralf hauled back quite a few chunks, and with the addition of some extra wood, they soon had a good blaze that took the chill out of the air. They ate some of the dried meat and sipped water sparingly. Most of the talk was subdued, as everyone was weary after a long day.

"I'll take the first watch," Ralf volunteered as he hunkered down by the fire with a section of old Aurochs horn he had freed up and his knife. His aching ribs would not allow him to sleep right away, and so he decided to sit up and hollow the thing out. The big Viking also had noted that the fog had drawn in closer to the shoreline, and that their ship had not been anchored nearby. So while the others rolled themselves in their cloaks and furs, he sat fashioning a blowing horn for summoning the ship.

It never occurred to any of Sinbad's landing party in the cave that night that the Blue Nymph and her crew might be lost to them. They were expecting to see her indigo sail and shapely figurehead namesake off the coast at anchor in the morning, but in truth she was drifting somewhere lost in the thick bank of fog between them. This fog was not just a visual impediment, but also a barrier between the warm and subtropical world that they had come from, and the land of fire and ice of long ago, both of which could not exist in the same time. This frozen land was a world they had willingly entered, but would not escape as easily.

Rafi sought out Omar as soon as he had recovered his composure. It was now afternoon, and the acting captain was admonishing a crew member who had just come down from the crows nest, lamenting that there was no land in sight and so he would never see the beautiful women of Karachi again.

"Well?" the thoroughly aggravated first mate said after he sent the distraught man below to get some rest.

"Please forgive an old man for his softening of the brain, but I do have something we can try. We will need your young friend up there with his pipes, but if Haroun can play that tune that mighty Ralf sang the night we found this land, he might be able to guide us back."

"He would not know the words," Omar pointed out in a blunt tone.

"No, he would not," Rafi admitted with measured patience, "but Haroun is good at capturing the spirit of a song. If he can repeat the tune with the same intensity of feeling, it might open the way once more."

"Might? So much uncertainty." Omar spat off the side.

"It holds more promise than what we face now. If we see but a glimpse of land, I trust you are enough sailor to be able to set course for it?" Rafi queried with an edge to his voice. It was after all, a fresh idea, and a better one than endlessly checking the same calculations over and over to no avail.

Omar stood with legs apart and hands balled on his hips, looking for all the world like a barrel on a stand with side handles. He laughed, but it was mirthless.

"I am Sindhi, and we are born of the sea. I have been a sailor all my life. Yet, you tell me that if this Pashtun bastard can play a heathen song on his wailing pipes, the land of fire and ice will just suddenly appear? That's nonsense!"

"You have tried this already?" Rafi asked quietly, and he raised an eyebrow at Omar's dismissal of his theory. Other men had begun to gather around, wondering what these two were arguing about now. There was a sense of uneasy desperation amongst them, and Omar knew he had to do something.

"No, I have not tried such an outlandish idea. It is most likely a waste of time, but time costs nothing out here, where we make no progress. If the boy can play it, let him try, and we will see what can be seen."

"Haroun!" went up the cry from many a throat. None out-sounded the booming voice of Omar. "Get up here boy, and bring that infernal noisemaker with you." In moments flapping bare feet were heard coming down the deck as the out-of-breath young man ran up with his pipes in hand.

"Yes, Omar," he said with a bow. "How can I serve you today?"

Omar frowned down at him, thinking he was being mocked, but the rebuke died on his lips as crew members eager to see what plan their acting captain had come up with began to gather round with hope dawning in their eyes.

"Useless One, can you play that mournful wailing that the Northern giant sang the night we journeyed here?"

Haroun's eyes lit up with excitement—Omar was actually asking him to play his pipes? "Oh, you mean the song about the frozen lands where the mountains shoot fire into the sky? I know some of it."

Rafi put a hand on his shoulder and bent low so only Haroun would hear. "Then play boy, and put your entire heart and soul into it, for otherwise we may never see our wise and generous captain and our other friends again."

"I'll play and I'll guide us back," Haroun promised, before he turned and ran to the main mast. He climbed like the monkey Omar often called him, quickly going up the tarry rigging, and hopped into the basket atop. He pulled the wooden pipes out of his sash, and with a few trial notes, began a fair approximation of the song that he had heard Ralf sing. "I only know the part it begins with, because I fell asleep after that," he called down uneasily.

"Just play what you know," Rafi called back up in his reedy old voice, while Omar fumed and cursed under his breath about lazy boys and their stupid inability to remain awake.

Haroun did play it, over and over, while the crew watched and prayed to Allah to be delivered of this evil. No one knew if it was the prayers or the mournful tune, or perhaps a combination of both; with so many souls aboard begging to be sent safely back to the place where they had left their most charming and capable captain and the three other people they trusted most to get them out of trouble. Suddenly, a gust of wind sprang up, and the sail flapped and filled as men cheered and crawled like spiders into the rigging to adjust the angle and tie down the lines to take advantage of the steadier breeze. There was a strange pressure in their ears at a change in the direction they were headed. The Blue Nymph began to slip through the water once more, with the fog parting around her bow.

Tentatively at first, and wavering ever so much, twin beams of faint but unmistakable radiance shone out from the figurehead as it literally breasted the waves.

"Keep playing boy!" Omar called out as Haroun had to take a break for a moment to hack and spit. Someone sidled over on the spar nearest and handed him a skin of watered wine, and he took a grateful sip before attacking the pipes with great fervor. Ahead of them now was a thinner layer of fog, with the faint sight of a nighttime ocean beyond. It did hold some bobbing ice, but did not look quite right.

"I fear we have come to some other frozen place," Omar said quietly to Rafi, who stood nearby. The taller man had also felt some uneasiness about the unfamiliar look of the approach. Until they cleared the fog, they would not be able to see if there was land beyond it.

"Things do appear different, but note that it is night here, and was still daylight when we left. Give it time; we can always go back and try again," Rafi counseled.

"If these men have the heart for that," Omar retorted darkly. "Who knows what monsters of the deep will come for us this time!"

"Omar, we are in deeper water than we had before," said a man at the bow who had been throwing a sounding lead. "Is it a channel?"

"I'm sure it is Basim. It will make our way easier," Omar said in his most encouraging tone. "Slow and steady ahead, and watch out for those chunks of ice that are bigger below than atop." If only his misgivings matched his ability to lie and bolster spirits, he might convince himself he was in the same icy shallow sea they had left previously.

As was their custom on strange shores, everyone slept with favored weapons near at hand. Ralf had finally gone to his rest, after waking Henri. Henri in turn awakened Tishimi, for they had decided to let Sinbad sleep the longest. All had noted how the captain had tossed half the night, his sleeping mind filled with thoughts of the treasure in the cave behind theirs, and how best to retrieve it.

In the predawn hours, the female samurai crouched alone at the fire, feeding it bits of kindling to get another couple chunks of old bone to catch and burn. She frowned when she saw it was nearly out, for Henri must have dozed and let it burn down too far. She soon had a decent blaze going again, and satisfied with that, she threw on two chunks of bone before she stood up and stretched.

Having an urgent need to relieve her bladder and wanting to watch the sun rise, she went outside the cave opening in the wan light of a new day, and tended to the first priority. The fur leggings with their easily removable center flap made that much easier, and only exposed her tender skin briefly to the biting cold. She was in the process of tying that back up again when she heard the growl from somewhere on the cliff top. Glancing up, all she could see was the quickly withdrawn form of something very large and vaguely catlike that had been crouching there. All thoughts of meditating in that harshly cold and dangerous area fled as she hurried back inside to see if the others were ready to rise.

Sinbad was up, stretching and yawning. Tishimi told him of her encounter as they made a cold morning meal of chewy dried meat washed down with tepid water.

"Let us hope we do not encounter it as we ascend again to retrieve our ivory," he said in a low voice that was not supposed to wake Ralf, but did.

"What—we have something else that wants to kill us?" the big Viking inquired as he sat up stiffly and scrubbed the sleep from his eyes. Sinbad and Tishimi filled him in on the scant details as he yawned and stretched, trying not to wince at the pain in his chest. He yawned cavernously and reached over to shake a snoring Henri.

"Wake up little man, your advice is needed," Ralf said in his booming voice. "Otherwise we will be forced to use you as bait."

Henri groaned and rolled over. "I will be glad to be back on board, where I am not sleeping on cold stone," he complained as he levered himself up to a sitting position. "All this walking makes a man tired."

"It would not be so cold if you had not let the fire go down while you napped on watch," Tishimi pointed out as Henri stumbled outside to answer nature's call.

"I kept one eye open," he retorted.

"Watch out for the giant cat, he might think you look like a good breakfast," Ralf chided him.

Henri wasted no time getting back indoors. "There is something prowling around up there, I could hear it snuffling. It is probably the chamber of death which draws it."

"Then we must be extra cautious in our climb today, for with what Tishimi has told me, this cat was the size of the lions of my father's land," Sinbad said as he rose gracefully to his full height and girded himself with his scimitar and dagger. Saeed's sword he tucked into the back of the cavern where it should not be easily found. "That is a very large animal, and quite dangerous. Weapons close, and be on your guard at all times," he added as he slipped out into the daylight, the others not far behind.

Ralf smothered the fire and covered it well, ensuring some coals would survive the day, making it easier to light in evening. He squeezed through the narrow opening last again, cursing to himself as he banged his head while trying to protect his ribs. "Let us hope that the next land we sail to has giants, so I won't have to stoop and crawl into every blasted doorway!"

They had to clamber back down onto the beach, and walked along it for the better part of an hour to access the narrow zigzagging trail up to the top of the bluffs. It was the easiest and safest way to climb. Looking out over the ocean as they trooped along, Sinbad grew troubled. Plenty of ice floes and a few icebergs floated out there, but there was no sign of the Blue Nymph. The tide was in, and had the ship experienced an accident, there would surely be some flotsam. They wouldn't have just sailed away and given their captain and his companions up for dead after just a few days away. It was a good crew, and Omar was like a brother. Something else must have happened.

If they had more wood, he would build a signal fire on the beach. Right now though, Sinbad had to turn his mind toward the climb ahead. Should one of those big cats—or any of that unfriendly local tribe—accost them while on that narrow and winding switchback, they would be in a precarious situation, regardless of whether they wound up fighting or retreating.

They had no impediment to their ascent until they reached the final yards, where one of the travois had somehow shifted and blocked access to the path. Sinbad reached up to shove it back and it moved far too easily. His heart sank as he came to the top of the bluff, and he swore audibly.

"What is the matter?" Henri called up, bow already in hand with an arrow in the other.

"We have been robbed in the night," Sinbad called back down in a frustrated tone. The travois poles were still there, though two of the four had been cut apart. The ivory, so long and hard fought for, was gone. Ralf came up behind him, with Tishimi and Henri hustling in the rear. They all looked around in dismay.

"Holy Odin, who took our cache?" the Viking boomed, fire in his eyes and his axe already in hand.

"It wasn't a big cat," Sinbad said sourly. He initially suspected it was the men who had come with them from the hunter's village, which were friendly with Varg of the Black Fur. If so, why hadn't they simply have taken the travois to haul it back? And how could only two men carry so much?

Ralf obviously had the same idea, for he started back the way they came. Henri had squatted next to something that interested him. Tishimi looked off down the bluff's edge toward where the sinkhole and their cave should be beneath it, but she couldn't make out anything but rocks and scrub that could have hidden several large predators or a couple dozen warriors.

Henri got to his feet and walked bent over, following some barely distinguishable signs. He beckoned them all to him, and pointed to several scuff marks. "It would seem that a party of perhaps seven to eight men came here, and they carried off our ivory." Sinbad hunkered down beside him, and the experienced hunter pointed to the signs of a raiding party in patchy snow and ice. "They wear a different sort of boot, like soft wrapped hide, for the sole leaves a wide and spread out print. You see here they walk in lightly, but over there, they leave heavily burdened. A man will move his feet apart and bend a little backwards to press deeper in the heel when he is carrying something of great weight."

He looked up, squinting at the sun's position in the sky.

"This trail is fresh, from dawn perhaps. We can follow them, at least," Henri said encouragingly, "They came up several hours behind us, and waited over there," he pointed to a patch of scrub, "Yet they did not go back the same way, nor did they use this trail we just ascended. They started out parallel along this bluff, heading past where we were staying last night."

"So they had been following us," said Sinbad thoughtfully. Looking off down the projected pathway, he wondered if perhaps there would be another way down to either the plains or the beach that would be easier to ascend as they went farther along the edge. The bluff curved in where their cave was, and then thrust forward not too far beyond it, forming sort of jutting promontory that was hard to see around. There could be other caves beyond that, he reasoned, and some of those might be inhabited.

Tishimi looked up at the sky. "If we in turn chase down these thieves, we will lose much of the day and then we will most likely have to fight. With so much other ivory lying untouched below, is it worth the trouble?"

Sinbad considered for a moment, his arresting blue eyes narrowed and distant. "Perhaps not, but I do not enjoy being robbed," he answered. "We saw no sign of these men when we left the ivory here, but they obviously saw us. They took our stockpile rather than scavenging for their own, when there is plenty available in that sinkhole. They had to know about that. Well, I for one fought too hard to obtain that ivory, so I want it back."

"I'll second that," Ralf rumbled, his axe in hand and a smoldering fury in his ice blue eyes.

"So then we will fight once again," Tishimi said in resignation, as her hands emerged from the long-furred sleeves of her parka to finger her swords.

"Lead on, Henri," Sinbad insisted, and the little man from Gaul went before them.

It took over an hour of following slowly behind Henri as he quartered back and forth, tracking the thieving men's progress. He lost the trail several times, and almost gave up in disgust, just before they came across a body. It lay half-covered in hastily scratched up snow and debris on the other side of a boulder, not too far from an unused spear. Initially Henri believed there had been a dispute, but since all the ivory had been dropped, and there was ample sign of others fleeing, he pulled the body free and rolled him over.

He was a stranger and a different sort of human. Short and stocky, he had a barrel chest, powerful limbs, and an oddly shaped face with a large nose, no chin, and a sloping skull with prominent brow ridges. There were deep gashes in his rough fur cape that went through his neck. Some blood had pooled beneath the body, but it was otherwise untouched.

"A dwarf!" Ralf said with surprise in his voice. He looked down and around with awe. "Maybe this is one of the Nine Realms after all."

"Nonsense! He is one of those flat-faced people the villagers spoke of," Henri told them. "This is just a boy on the cusp of manhood," he told them, pointing out the scraggly wisps of beard. "Still he must have been very strong and powerful for his height and weight, to have carried such a heavy load. He was taken by surprise, for any man built like him with such a weapon as that heavy spear would not otherwise die so easily."

"So these are young men who stole our ivory?" Sinbad asked in an incredulous tone, squatting beside Henri to peer at the strangely shaped youth.

"Yes," Henri confirmed, looking around speculatively. "Perhaps he and his friends sought glory for themselves by tracking and raiding from us. They likely sent out a scout, the main party waiting until we were out of sight and hearing before they came back and took our ivory. This all happened since sunrise though. He is not frozen or even very stiff." Henri lifted an arm, which was still somewhat limp. "The blood beneath him is still sticky. It was no more than two to three hours past."

"Do you know what killed him?" Sinbad asked with a speculative frown.

"He is one of the flat-faced people…"

Henri met his gaze levelly. "I would say from the way his neck is slashed and broken, it was the same sort of predator that ended Saeed's life. It is big," he added, pointing out the telltale signs of jugular crushing. "It did not kill him here, but dragged him off from somewhere nearby. The men with him fought, but they abandoned their friend when another big creature came in from that direction," he said, pointing to the edge of the bluff. "The two beasts did not fight over the kill, so perhaps are a mated pair."

"Tigers and leopards will drag their prey," Sinbad said, drawing his sword and thinking of the big cat Tishimi saw. "Yet they hunt alone. Lions hunt in prides. Some of them do cache their excess meat."

"So do bears drag food, and they too will save it for a later time, but they do not bite this way. Whatever killed this man, I do not think it is something we have ever seen, for it has teeth like curved knives. If it stored his body, is not nearby now, but it intends to come back."

They all looked around with concern. This was an upland area above the plains, with some taller brush, stunted and windblown trees, and many large rocks that were hard to see through. Unless the creature was tall like the mammoths, there was enough cover that it could be on them in moments.

"The others with him ran away in great fear," Henri pointed out. "They have not come back for this ivory they so coveted, or for the body of their companion."

"Well there is little we can do for him, and his interment is the business of his own people. Let us get this ivory out of here, and then we can figure out some way to get it back down to the beach," Sinbad said as he stood again. As an afterthought, he placed the man's spear beside him, as a sign of respect. Ralf approved.

"He was a thief, but this is a harsh land. A warrior should lie with his weapon at hand," he said in benediction.

The four bundles of tusk sections had been dropped at random spots, and one of them had split open, making it harder to carry. Ralf hefted one, grunting a bit, but he thought he could carry it back the way they had come. With a similar groan Sinbad grabbed up another and staggered forward. Tishimi and Henri hefted a third between them, but they would not make good progress that way.

"I cannot... haul this much weight... and stay on my feet very long..." Henri said, puffing.

"You... are... weak," Tishimi insisted, but she was straining every muscle trying to keep up with him.

"Set it... all down. Let us bring back... what we can... this trip. You two... guard our way." Sinbad insisted. But even he gave in after a dozen more steps.

"This... isn't working. I have... a better idea," the big Viking said in an equally strained voice as he set his bundle down. It took him a moment to catch his breath. "If we lash the remaining ivory to poles... we will be able to carry it between us far easier. Maybe even... all the way down that trail," he wheezed. He was short of breath again, and every deep drawn one hurt in his chest.

"That's a workable idea," Sinbad said from where he stood looking back the way they had come. "If you can go back for several of those poles and some of the lashings, Tishimi, Henri, and I can collect the other scattered bundle and carry it here."

"I'll be back within the hour," the Viking promised. Ostensibly recovered, he headed off with a long-legged, ground eating stride that would get him to where they had been robbed faster than carrying a hundred fifty pounds of ivory would.

"Let's go collect that other ivory before those big tooth cats show up again," Sinbad insisted. With Henri complaining all the way, they set off again for where they had left the body of the stranger and the scattered pieces of mammoth tusk.

Even with three of them, it was still quite a chore moving that much ivory. They weren't gasping and staggering under their burdens as they had earlier, but it took two trips to do it safely. By the end of the second trip, when all the cut pieces of mammoth tusk were together once more, they took a rest and some refreshment in chewy dried meat and sips of spring water.

"It is late in the afternoon," Henri observed, squinting up at the sky. "We will face darkness again going down that trail if we don't soon get this heavy stuff back to where we left it."

"Ralf should be back here shortly," Sinbad insisted. He had expected to see the Viking coming an hour ago. Knowing Ralf, he had tried to haul everything at once, and with his bruised chest, got winded again. Sinbad got to his feet. "I'm going to set out and see if I can give him a hand. Guard this for now, and if we are not back in an hour, leave the ivory and make for the trail down. I'll not risk you both to predators you cannot see at night," he added, thinking about the bear that had attacked them at the village as he set off.

"I will be glad when we are back aboard the ship. I am tired of being cold," Henri complained.

"No more than the rest of us," Tishimi agreed. She fingered the bear tooth necklace and thought of Doh Brom, who had always lived this life; and of Farhad, who insisted on staying. "I hope our next voyage is to somewhere warm."

"I do not like being exposed like this," Henri admitted. "Anything can creep up on you."

The winds sweeping up off the plains below had a mournful sound that rattled in the brush around them. "You cannot hear a mouse rustling with this accursed wind," she agreed.

"No, but there are other signs of a large predator advancing. Birds will fly up or suddenly go quiet, and the small creatures will scramble to get out of the way."

There was a long, watchful, and uneasy silence between them before the sound of voices came from the direction of where Sinbad had set out. Henri climbed a rock and shaded his eyes against the low-slanting afternoon sun. "It is Sinbad and Ralf, and they have the wood and travois—all of it. We may get out of here tonight after all." He waved and whistled, trying to gain their notice lest they inadvertently walked past.

"Hen-ree," Tishimi said quietly, for she had heard a slight rustle behind them, and turned around to see what was making it. "I fear we have attracted some unwanted attention!" Her blades came out with the soft ring of fine metal on the light wood of the saya they rested in.

The hunter spun around, his bow already in hand and an arrow drawn, but instead of the small, burly, flat faced men he had expected, what he saw made the hair stand up on the back of his neck. No more than a few running steps behind them crouched a scimitar cat. Nearly four feet high at the shoulder, and fully ten feet long to the stubby tail, it had a high front end that sloped down to lower hindquarters. The coat was thick and light tawny spotted with pale black freckles with partial stripes on the legs, shading to cream underneath. It blended in beautifully with the snow dotted rocky upland. The most arresting feature though was the large head with protruding dagger-edged upper teeth that curved back into pockets on either side of the lower lips. It stood there as if mesmerized, audibly snuffling in their direction and watching them warily with big amber eyes.

It had come up on them with no warning, and if not for its curiosity about these new humans, they would not have lived to see it.

Henri let loose, but the big creature ducked and turned, almost seeming to disappear. It was more interested in the men coming up behind them, and had melted back into the brush to stalk around the two smaller beings in order to get between them and Sinbad and Ralf. These puny ones could be hunted down later, but the bigger two legged one was a threat that must be dealt with, so close to the den.

Henri spun around to follow its movements, and noted two more shadows to the far side of them stalking by, also headed in the direction that Ralf and Sinbad came from. He let loose at the nearest one, but the range was too distant. He could not tell if it was hit when it suddenly dropped to a crouch. A fourth one was already circling around to the outside of the two unwary men, who were chatting amiably as they dragged their burdens along, and a fifth came in from behind. The idea was clear; trap these two-legged beasts between them, and then take one or both of them down.

For once, even usually overcautious Henri didn't pause. "Sinbad, Ralf, big cats, look out!" he yelled as he sprang down and ran into their action, his bow twanging as he drew and released, scoring two non-fatal hits out of three shots. One cat limped off snarling and biting at its flank. The other went down rolling, but came back up and turned to race directly at Henri, who was already taking careful aim, awaiting the perfect shot to drop it. It was nearly atop him before he let fly with first one and then another arrow, and barely scrambled out of the way in time to avoid being flattened as the body in mid-leap dropped like a boulder, two arrows bristling from its mouth and throat.

Tishimi went racing past him with both katana and wakizashi drawn, her warbling war cry echoing eerily off rocks and brush as she picked out a giant cat-like form loping ahead before it also decided to turn on the small man from Gaul. Of Sinbad's current party, she was the fastest, but these big animals had great speed, so she could not keep up. Sinbad and Ralf were already engaged in a fight with their own adversaries, so she concentrated on keeping this wounded one busy, feinting in and out, hoping to get in a few blows here and there. She might not be able to kill it, but if she sliced it often enough, blood loss should slow it until it either dropped of exhaustion, or she could get close enough to get in a fatal stab. She darted back and forth before it, her blades flashing in the afternoon sunlight, her attention solely on the creature she was facing off against. It circled and batted at her like a great house cat with a mouse. This mouse however had sharp and shining weapons that cut and let blood flow freely. One of them would win, but it was never certain if it would be the big feline with the curved teeth, who crouched prepared to leap forward and crush down this small but determined two legged pest, or the completely focused warrior woman who would never give in until her enemy expired.

Their dance of death seemed to slow time, and it took such concentration, not even the whiz of a passing arrow broke her concentration. Tishimi was almost disappointed when the first shaft buried itself in the muzzle of the beast, temporarily fusing it shut, and the next went deep into the chest as it sprang up in surprise. The second shot was perfectly placed, and the big cat took several wobbling steps forward before it slumped to the ground dead in its tracks.

"I would have beat it," she said with a slight edge to her voice as Henri stepped up beside her. Her eyes narrowed at him as he grinned over at her.

"If looks could kill, we would all be just as dead," he quipped, but then spotted something just beyond their two beleaguered friends.

Henri pointed. "Another big cat and I am out of arrows!"

The two big men had dropped their burdens and ran forward to be clear of the poles. Both blade and axe came immediately to hand. They positioned themselves back to back, beset on more than one side, waiting for the two cats that were stalking them to rush in. They had not noticed the one behind them yet.

Mighty Ralf was singing his war song as gaily as if this was a sparring session. His narrowed eyes were fixed on one huge feline form racing at him with all thoughts of previous injuries forgotten in his blood lust to pit himself against such a monster. Two handed, his axe swung out and back in great arcs, as he chopped at the beast. It was circling him warily, looking for a chance to use its superior weight and speed to bear him down. He was getting winded quickly though; his chest still swollen inside from the pounding he had taken during the mammoth hunt and all the hard work since. When it finally saw an opening and jumped at him, the mass movement behind three hundred and seventy-five pounds of cat hitting him in the chest knocked the wind from him.

On battle instinct alone, while gasping for air he lashed out and cut off part of a fore paw that slapped at him. The big cat screeched as it fell away backwards, but still managed to come up on three legs, snarling as he scrambled to his feet. As its head jutted forward with those huge teeth bared defiantly in his face, Ralf's axe swung high and came down with a crash on the skull. It dropped like a stone.

"They fall as hard as they hit you," he exclaimed with a wheeze and a grim smile, as he turned to see if Sinbad needed help. He still did not see the fifth cat circling behind him, holding back while it waited for a distracted moment to rush in.

Sinbad had picked out an adversary of his own. Shucking his parka, he tensed and smiled grimly, his blade ready to sing out as soon as the beast got close enough. He had seen lions hunted before with spears, but never with a sword. This big cat had a strange shape with far more deadly looking canine teeth, curved in a way that reminded him of his own crescent blade. *Allah be willing, let this be a first then, that a man kill a lion with only a blade,* he prayed as he leapt forward to meet the creature's rush, his scimitar flashing in arcs and curves that cut bloody swathes into its legs, face, and chest. Red spatters went everywhere and the creature roared and drooled all over him as they both fought desperately for supremacy. Its weight was its primary advantage up close, because those curving, slashing teeth were thin, and would break if they encountered thick bone.

Sinbad was no long-bodied bison or deer to be attacked from behind, and he was armed with a curved cutting surface of his own that he understood the use of as well as the cat knew its own weapons. He was fast, but it was faster, and eventually the great forelegs wrapped around him with the single curved dewclaw on each front paw digging in painfully to his sides as it wrestled him down. Yet Sinbad was not one to give up no matter how dreadful the odds, so ignoring the pain, he brought his arms up with sword in hand. Before the open mouth could bring those four inch curved and sharply serrated canine teeth into play, he plunged the tip of his blade into the throat and twisted it into a sideways slice.

Another bubbling roar as blood sprayed from the torn jugular, and the cat let go as it went down almost atop him. Sinbad found himself trapped beneath the body, which was still twitching and jerking as it died. Ralf set aside his axe to lend him a hand, and that is when the fifth cat struck.

Tishimi started running as soon as she noted the additional danger. The big animal that had hung back now raced directly at Ralf, and before she could get to him, it bore him down, face first. The weight of it pressed on his bruised chest and cracked ribs and he gasped for air again before blacking out. Its head came down for the fatal bite to the back of the neck

Sinbad was a captive witness to the entire thing, as he tried desperately to squirm out from under the dead scimitar cat that had landed atop him. He was in no position to help his friend, for he had lost track of his own weapon in the struggle, but he would have fought it with hands and teeth had he been free. Before the big beast could get in a killing bite though, Tishimi was there, flashing her blades in its face. Its attention off Ralf for the moment, it snarled and batted at her, catching her parka and ripping it half free. She pulled away and the warm jacket remained behind, caught in the dewclaw of the big animal that shook its forefoot to loosen the flapping bit of fur before turning its attention back to Ralf, who was just coming to, now that the weight had shifted.

Ralf was able to shove the creature sideways off balance, but before he could bring his axe up, it had him pinned down again. Henri had run in with his knife drawn, but it was Tishimi who ended the siege. With the grace and lithe balance of a dancer, she leapt up onto the cat's back. It bucked and reared at the unaccustomed weight like a wild horse, though unlike a horse it could easily twist sideways to go over onto its back in an attempt to crush her. It squirmed bonelessly, trying to reach her with front paws or rake her with hind claws, but she moved with it and ignored the discomfort, which was scraping her legs painfully beneath the fur leggings. With grim determination, Tishimi crossed both swords in the front of its neck and ripped the deadly sharp opposing blades across its throat. Before it could fall over and trap her beneath it, she tossed her weapons free and vaulted off sideways, hitting the ground crouched and ready to run.

The cuts were not as deep as she would have liked, but they were deep enough. The big cat slowly raised back up on all fours and staggered forward with a dull and dazed look as showers of bubbling blood ran down its chest. It gave one feeble sniff before it slumped sideways and fell heavily, dead.

"That... that was... truly magnificent!" Henri exclaimed as he rushed over to help the battered and shivering woman to her feet.

"You made some amazing shots," she said through clenched and chattering teeth, partly due to the cold, and partly because the battle nerves were wearing off.

"Here, take my coat," Henri said gallantly. "I have leathers underneath." He quickly undid it and dropped it over her shoulders. For once, she did not fight with him about his off-and-on sense of chivalry, and he even got a shy, if shaky smile.

Ralf was dazedly regaining his own feet before staggering over to help Sinbad extricate himself.

"Five great lions from one pride, all killed without spears. That is something we will be bragging about to our grandchildren," their smiling if similarly clawed and bruised leader said with amazement as he regained his feet. "Allah has been merciful today." He winced a bit at the wounds in his sides, which were deep and painful.

"The gods smile on the valorous," Ralf agreed. "Let no man or woman ever say our company is not the bravest of the brave. We should take trophies to prove our story," he added, looking over the big cats curiously. Henri was going around extracting his least damaged arrows. He wound up with only two that could be reused, which made him frown. "Their pelts would make magnificent rugs."

Henri bent over one, and took a few experimental cuts. "It will take a long time to skin out these hides with just our knives," he complained.

"Perhaps tomorrow," Sinbad insisted. "It is more important that we move the ivory while we still have some light left. Tishimi and Henri, you will be our guards. Ralf and I will do the hauling. If we work quickly, we should get most of it down on the beach by dark."

While they bundled the ivory to carry off again, Henri took a few moments to knock out and remove the big serrated teeth from each of the big cats' mouths. These he threw into his belt pouch, with thoughts of stringing them later as trophies, for if predators got to the cats before they came back to claim them, the pelts would be ruined.

It did take them the rest of the day, with bundles of heavy sections of tusk lashed first to travois, and then swinging from double poles carried on broad shoulders, but the ivory was eventually hauled down to the beach, and hidden beneath their upturned boat. They brought the wood down too. The work was hard and tiring, for even those who weren't carrying anything had to trek up and down the narrow and twisting trail, and all were exhausted after a day of battling predators and the elements. The last loads were carried in arms in the dark, with only small sputtering torches to light the way. Tishimi was able to retrieve her torn parka, and Henri promised to show her how to re-lace it once they were under cover for the night.

The one thing each of the four members of the shore party had noted, but had not commented on as they went to their weary repose in the cave that would shelter them for yet another night was the absence of the Blue Nymph. What good would all their hard work be, along with the injuries that had been sustained, if they had no way to return to their own world? What use were riches in ivory when you were left behind in a land of fire and ice, to live out your days like some savage? Water was abundant enough, but without food and proper shelter, they would not survive long. Certainly the villagers would take them in again, but each restless heart longed to be back on the open sea, and off to further adventures. It was a weary and disconsolate foursome that dropped off to sleep that night without even bothering to post a guard.

Morning dawned bright and clear behind the Blue Nymph. They were able to sail carefully into the outer part of a sheltered bay, though it was narrow and bobbing with ice, and hemmed in by promontories on both sides. No landing spot here, but several squat men dressed in furs with tangled hair and beards watched them warily from a cave partway up the cliffs. They were holding heavy spears and did not look friendly, and more than one crew member hoped Sinbad and his company had not run afoul of these savage-looking strangers.

The closer in toward land they came, the more the shoreline appeared somewhat similar to the one they had left behind; only rockier and less accessible to even a small craft. They continued to sail on, but nothing seemed familiar, and the cliffs rose steeply off the ice-choked water below. They passed an ice field that flowed all the way down to the water's edge, and the glaciers that had spawned it seemed far closer now. It felt like they had gone too far north.

Omar was still unsure of himself, for that time in the fog with the sun on the wrong side had unnerved him. Even if this was the same landmass, their initial approach to it had been from the southeast. He decided to trust his instincts that this sector was likely in the northeast of the same land, so they were sailing in the opposite direction.

"We are heading the wrong way," he told the man at the tiller after ordering the sail changed. "Set our course due south along this coastline, but stay far enough out to sea that we don't bottom out. Allah be willing, we will find the beach where they landed. If not, we will perhaps send the other small boat out, and they will build a fire ashore to signal Sinbad that we are back. The only other thing we can do is pray."

Let us hope that we have landed in the same time period, let alone the same place, Rafi was thinking as the Blue Nymph gradually came around. He stood on the port side toward the stern, wrapped in a wool cloak, watching the unfamiliar landscape they were passing. Once again as the day grew longer, the fog had begun to roll in behind them. At least now, the sail fulled and the ship cut the waves as the nautical miles slipped away.

Going *somewhere* was far better than going nowhere at all.

It was a dismal night, for as cheerful as the fire was and as successful as they had been in their fight with the scimitar cat pride along with the retrieval of the ivory, two of them were seriously injured now. Tishimi's scratches were superficial, as she had still worn the thick leggings, but Sinbad's puncture wounds from the cat claws had gone deep through skin into underlying muscle, and now showed some signs of infection. Tishimi did what she could for him, and both Henri and Ralf gave advice on what herbs and leaves to try as poultices. Yet no matter what she steeped in a few shells hastily cleaned in fresh snow and filled with meltwater, the deep puncture wounds puffed and began to look angry red, and by the time they went to sleep, were already edged with yellow pus. Sinbad laughed it off as no more than scratches, but by morning he was running a fever and had the chills. The glands under his arms and neck were swollen, indicating the infection had entered his bloodstream.

"I do not know what else to do for him," Tishimi told the others. They knew Rafi would have a remedy, but the knowledgeable elder man was on the Blue Nymph, and that was nowhere in sight.

"It is just a couple of scratches," Sinbad insisted, but he was drinking a lot of water, and he seemed weak and shaky. By the time they left the shelter to check on the ivory, he was dizzy and staggering as he tried to follow them. "Perhaps I just need more sleep," he told Ralf, who steered him back into the cave.

"Set our course due south along this coastline..."

"Build up the fire, we'll sweat it out of him," the Viking said with surety. Both he and Sinbad had seen far worse war wounds over the years, some of which did fester. Allowed to go too far, the infection began to attack a man from the inside. "Then go down by the boat, and guard our ivory. We don't want anyone stealing that again. Build a signal fire maybe, a good smoky one that can be seen from a distance. Take some bone with you, and some embers from in here," Ralf added.

"What will you do here while we are gone?" Henri asked with irritation. He had managed to make himself two more arrows from the leavings of others and turned some brush shaved with his knife into shafts, but he was out of sinew to bind them and they had no fletching. They would only fly at close range. Four arrows would not be much protection against man nor beast anyway.

"I'm going to tell Sinbad a story while he rests," the Viking answered as he heated the tip of his knife in the fire until it was red hot.

"Go on then, and just leave us be," Sinbad said weakly, but even so, his voice held a note of command.

Tishimi bowed, and Henri raised a hand, and they left to go keep busy. Once they were out of earshot, the two men had a low-voiced conversation.

"You know what I have to do, Sinbad," Ralf said in a quiet rumble as he approached his leader with the white hot knife tip. "If we don't get that poison out and seal those wounds, you will be too sick to recover in another day."

"I know—just do it!" Sinbad said, shaking with chills as he shucked off his parka, pulled up his tunic, and rolled onto his side to present the first wound, which was ugly and raised, the reddened part purpling. Ralf handed him a peeled section of wood Henri had left behind and the captain gritted his teeth around it.

The initial wound was small, but so infected it was very swollen and went deep at an angle. It took some probing to get it all open. To Sinbad's credit, he did no more than gasp and groan as the fiery metal sank in, cutting all around to loosen the septic tissue. Blood and yellow pus gushed out, and Ralf let that run for a few moments while he reheated the knife to cauterize the wound. Sinbad had bitten well into the wood, and had to choose another spot or his teeth would saw clear through it.

"This one will scar," Ralf said as he applied the heated metal once more, and Sinbad winced. He never cried out though, even when the same procedure was done on the other side, which was mercifully less deep and somewhat smaller. When Ralf had finished, there were two arrow blanks that Henri would not find usable.

Ralf packed both spots with clean snow to sooth the open and seared flesh, and tied Sinbad's raggedy sash over them before helping his weary captain and companion back into his clothing.

"Thank you... my friend," Sinbad said in a faltering voice, as his eyes drifted closed. Ralf dropped one of the woolen capes over him.

"I just wish we'd had some ale," Ralf grumbled.

His captain opened one eye and gave a lopsided grin. "For me...or for... your... self?" he asked the Viking in a tired voice.

"Yes," was all Ralf said as he watched his best boon companion drift off to sleep.

"So we are to sit out in the cold doing nothing," Henri complained he and Tishimi made their way down toward the boat. There was a fog out at sea again, and they could not see much beyond the first half mile. No sign of the Blue Nymph.

"They wanted to get us out of there for a reason," Tishimi answered quietly as she followed his gaze.

"Of course, I understood that," he retorted testily. "The big one has some sort of drastic measure of healing in mind, and he did not want us to hear our captain cry out in pain," he added in a flippant tone. Henri was not a cruel man, but he shuddered at the thought of the hot knife slicing into sore and swollen flesh, and liked to believe that even Sinbad had his weaknesses.

Tishimi rounded on him, her eyes narrowed and her voice low and tight with fury.

"Sinbad does not *cry*, nor does he feel pain like other men. This I know, because I have fought beside him, and I have seen him far more seriously injured. Yet he still carried a wounded man from the heat of the battle, and he did not collapse until we were victorious. He even sewed shut his own cuts and sent the surgeon to help others. Two days and he was aboard ship again. He is stronger than anyone I know."

"You love him," Henri blurted, almost half accusingly. Something about that idea bothered him. Of the three men who were her companions, Henri had the hardest time accepting Tishimi as just another warrior. He knew her skills, and yet her femininity was always foremost in his mind.

The women of his homeland did not fight or hunt, and her independence was intriguing.

She had to clench and unclench her hands and breathe deeply before she replied. "I must remind you that I am Bushi—Samurai as it is known in foreign lands. I am a warrior of my people. Sinbad is my captain, my leader, and my friend. I will protect his honor and his life until I am no longer wanted or needed. I find your attitude insulting, Gaul."

He grunted noncommittally. She fingered the bear claw necklace Doh Brom had given her, and looked out over the ocean before glaring back at Henri.

"Perhaps in your homeland, *all* the women bow to men, and none of them will ever learn to protect themselves or each other. It is not so everywhere else. Many of our women are subservient as well, but I am not one of them, and you would do well to remember that."

"I did not mean to be insulting, just stating what seems to be evident," Henri said. "I think all of us admire Sinbad, and is that not a kind of love as well?" He had set out the pieces of old bone he'd carried down, and began casting around for driftwood, dried grass, and anything else that would feed a fire.

"I suppose," Tishimi admitted, and while she kept a hard edge to her voice, she turned away to help in the search for combustibles while Henri laid the fire and lit it. "I will forgive this disrespectful attitude for now, and assume it was a misunderstanding, but I do not wish to hear about 'love' again. I am wedded to my pledge." She looked up as she set something down, and noted Henri was watching her with hooded eyes over the small blaze he had successfully started. "I can have no other lovers but these." She patted the hilts of her swords.

"It will be a lonely life for you then," he said simply, as he stood up and turned away. She went to gather more bits of wood and some sedges, moss and other things that would make thick smoke, but spun around with her blades drawn when Henri cried out in surprise.

"Mon Dieu, what now?" he exclaimed.

As they approached the southern promontory that hemmed in the small bay, the Blue Nymph had to swing out to sea to avoid both rocks and ice. Basim had continued to use the sounding lead to keep them from bottoming out. The water was very shallow in areas that had previously been dry land when the glaciers had covered all the upper continent. It was their relentless march over the land that had carved the plains and ridges, valleys and drumlins, by the force of rock and soil the towering ice walls pushed ahead. Their gradual retreat left behind riverbeds, waterfalls, and the scars and debris of their previous advances and retreats.

As mankind spread over the tundra plains, the era of giant creatures and year-long winters was slowly passing away. However, to the crew aboard the Blue Nymph, who were used to tropical climes and warm breezes, it was cold enough to require protective clothing and men still shivered as they went about their duties. More than one voiced complaints, and concerns about how Sinbad and his company could have possibly survived in such a frozen landscape. Only Rafi and Haroun seemed to find it interesting, if somewhat forbidding.

All along the coast, seals and some walruses basked on rocks or larger ice floes within reach of the water. Men stared at the strange creatures with the long teeth and bulky bodies in surprise, for while some had seen seals in their travels, the great tusked walrus was virtually unknown. What wonders this land held!

Haroun was back in the crows-nest that afternoon, when his sharp eyes spotted a thin thread of smoke rising to the sky. It came from somewhere around the next bend. Unfortunately they would have to swing much farther out to sea to get there, as both jutting rocks and icebergs were in their way. If they did move beyond the fog, they would likely loose sight of the land again.

"Drop anchor here, we will send out the small boat to investigate," Omar decided. "For all we know, it might just be more of those savages. We do not dare risk leaving the shoreline before we are sure where we must go." He knew now that if they moved into the densest fog, they might not come back in the same spot. It would not set well with the crew if they lost sight of land again. For all these were hardy seamen used to being on trackless ocean waters; that dead zone between fog banks had thoroughly spooked them. They would not enter it willingly again without the charismatic influence of their amiable and enthusiastic captain to reassure them that all would be well.

Several men volunteered to man the small boat, and it was lowered over the side with the makeshift harpoon aboard in case they needed to defend themselves. Once the handpicked crew clambered down and set off, they moved far faster via oars than the Blue Nymph had been able to sail. For most of the exploration of the coastline, Omar had insisted they reef much of her canvas to keep to a cautious speed. The narrower and less deep hull of the rowboat could squeeze between obstacles with ease, and was soon out of sight as it passed around the edge of the promontory.

Several male walruses had been disturbed by something large passing by overhead as they fed on clams in the water around the tip of the promontory. Since their only regular predators at the time were killer whales or the white bears that frequented the frozen coastlines, they had swum over to the beach where Henri and Tishimi were, and slowly humped their way out of the water, using their tusks to pull themselves along. They weren't particularly concerned about these smaller, upright beasts, but faced out toward the open sea, growling and hooting to each other.

"What are those things?" Henri wondered aloud, walking slowly around them while keeping a proper distance. The biggest one eyed them balefully before rolling onto his back to scrub himself in the sand.

"Some sort of giant seal I would think," Tishimi said with inquisitive concern, from where she watched cautiously. "Yet I have never seen seals so large, or with such long teeth."

"Everything here seems to have some sort of horns or tusks. I wonder if these things are edible?" he added, reaching for his bow. Dried meat was running low and there was no sign of the Blue Nymph yet. Fresh food would be most welcome, and these flabby behemoths should taste better than day old dead cat.

"I would not get too close, they might decide to charge you," she warned as he stalked up to get within shooting range. She stopped well back, nervously intent on protecting her companion, yet also curious to see the results of his hunt.

"Oh please, these big lumps can barely move," he scoffed, as one of them raised its head, with its tusks in the air. Henri had no idea that this was an aggressive and threatening gesture. He was just about to fire when all three of the creatures heaved themselves up on their limbs and headed straight at him, humping along as quickly as he could move—which was surprisingly fast. He turned tail and sprinted off with the three of them right behind him. Had there just been the one, he would have stood his ground, but with only four arrows, there was the chance that he'd be overrun and gored by one as he tried to take down another.

Tishimi stood back, a half smile on her face. She could tell Henri was in no danger, for the big creatures would stop after a few minutes and regroup. It was good for the cocky little man to learn a lesson about arrogant pride. She shouted encouragement now and then as he tried to come around and take aim, but as soon as he approached the creatures started after him again, and on the open beach there was nowhere to hide.

After all they had been through in the past several days, it was comical to watch, and in spite of herself, Tishimi giggled so hard she had to hold her stomach. She had her back to the southern promontory, which is why she didn't see what else was coming around the bend, as Henri raced back and forth, alternately becoming the hunter and the hunted.

With Sinbad asleep, Ralf had stepped outside for a while, to sit in the wan sun sharpening his axe. Looking out over the water floating with ice, he was reminded once again of his homeland far away. Should the ship never come back for them, this would not be such a bad place to make a life. There were no domestic animals to farm, but plenty of hunting, and enough challenges and adventure to keep a man satisfied. The women were certainly free with their favors. With Sinbad here with him, he would be content.

There was a commotion down on the beach, and he set down his whetstone and stood up with axe in hand. When he saw what was going on, a knowing smile came across his face and he headed on down. Fresh meat was something they could use, and eating walrus was not unknown to his kinsman. Sinbad was asleep but his sword was nearby. Hopefully nothing would creep up on him while he slumbered.

Ralf was tired and sore, but he didn't consider walruses particularly hard to kill. While they were chasing Henri, he sprinted up behind the closest one and chopped down on the back of its head. The big animal dropped like a rock, and the other two panicked and went lumbering back out into the water.

"Give me a hand with this," Ralf called to Henri as he began lopping off parts. The smaller man from Gaul was winded, and he set down his bow and quiver to come over with his knife.

"These things can move fast," he commented breathlessly as he squatted next to Ralf, who had used his axe to groove a channel in the sand to run off the blood before settling down to butchering. The big Viking only grunted as he cut away thick skin and hunks of blubber, trying to get to the meat. He saved parts here and there, declaring them a delicacy, or somehow useful.

"At least we'll have fresh meat tonight," he half rumbled to himself. "Someone should go check on Sinbad though."

"I will do that." Tishimi had gone back to stoke the signal fire, and then turned to head back toward their sheltering cave. She was halfway down the beach when she called back softly, "Ralf, Hen-ree, a boat!"

Both men immediately regained their feet, bloody weapons already in hand. It was small craft, with men at oars. They were so far out, even sharp eyed Henri could not make out who they were. The Viking narrowed his eyes suspiciously.

"Go wake Sinbad!" he insisted, and she took off at a run.

Sinbad may have been ill and in pain, but he had warrior instincts. His sleeping brain knew dimly that Ralf had left the vicinity of the cave, and so that part of his mind which concentrated on self-preservation awakened him to the stealthy steps at the opening to the cave. He knew immediately they did not belong to anyone in his party. Still a bit weak and wobbly, he was nonetheless on his feet and armed fast enough to hear the retreat of soft booted feet just outside.

Sinbad slipped through the opening, and was amused to find five carefully folded scimitar cat pelts bundled together on the rock where Ralf had been sitting. On inspection, they had been hurriedly but expertly flayed, and while they would still require washing and tanning, there would be little in the way of scraping left. How long their benefactor had been watching them was unknown, but perhaps this was supposed to be some sort of tribute.

"Thank you, my friend," Sinbad said to the rocks around him, lifting his sword in a warrior's salute. A great commotion on the beach drew his attention, and that is when he saw Tishimi running his way. He began climbing down to meet her.

"Sinbad!" she called out breathlessly, "A small vessel has come, but I do not know if these are friend or foe."

"It will be from our ship," he reassured her as he caught up, still feeling a little weak and his injuries smarting, but grinning from ear to ear. "These primitive people have no such skills, nor do they have abundant wood. Omar sent our other boat out to look for us."

And so it was, that when hailed, the men from the Blue Nymph rowed to shore and there was a joyous reunion. Sinbad himself insisted on being rowed back to his ship so that he personally could man the tiller and guide it in as close as possible. By late afternoon, the Blue Nymph was once again anchored off the coast.

It took the better part of three more days and additional men to extricate, cut up, and carry out all the mammoth ivory that they could loosened from the sinkhole cave. It lay piled on the beach in heaps above the high tide, where they would load one boat and tow it with the other to get it aboard. Some horn and antlers were taken as well, and Ralf insisted on having the walrus tusks. Sinbad, feeling much better and proclaimed well on the way to being healed by Rafi, stood proudly before them, his eyes sparkling at the potential for a great profit.

"This will pay my crew well, and outfit us handsomely for our next voyage," he said in a jubilant tone to Ralf, who when not stacking or cutting ivory, had been working on creating his second horn. The first one had been donated to the Blue Nymph, to be used when in a fog, so that a shore party could actually hear them and know the location.

"Good, because when we get back, I am going to drink a barrel of rotgut wine, and buy myself several nights with a couple of eager wenches," the Viking bragged. He looked not at Sinbad, but up over the bluff toward the travois trail that lead to the village with the widowed sisters.

"You shall have it, my friend. In fact, I will pay for it all, as a boon for saving my life," Sinbad reassured him.

"Bah, keep your money," Ralf countered. "Life is cheap, but good companions you cannot buy. I'll likely need a loan sometime anyway." They both laughed.

In the meantime, under Henri's direction, two men helped him scrape, stretch, and preserve the hides of the five big cats on frames made from the wood of the travois. It was not enjoyable work, but the sailors involved reveled in the stories of the sights the landing party had seen and the adventures they had lived through. Henri himself managed to escape most of the dirty work by insisting he must make more arrows. During the evenings he worked on gently tapping the crescent teeth of the big cats, and stringing them two together on rawhide for his companions and himself. A broken off one he kept for Haroun, for the boy was fascinated with everything the little hunter from Gaul told him about his own exploits, and believed it no matter how outrageous the boasting became. The extra tooth he strung also and presented to Tishimi, to do with as she liked. "For saving the life of a giant in a most remarkable way," he told her.

Saeed it was found would not be greatly missed, though before they left, his sword would be ritually given to the icy waters. Farhad's decision to remain behind was mourned mostly by the younger members of the crew. "The girl he chose to espouse was a beauty, and they are happy together," Sinbad reassured everyone. "He thrives on this sort of life." Everyone wished him well.

Tishimi spent much of her time helping wherever she was needed, but often found herself alone with her thoughts. Even amongst her closest companions, she was still very much a loner. She thought of Doh Brom often, and wished there was some way she could thank the elder woman for her wisdom and her companionship. In the end, she decided to leave some sort of message behind. Begging ink from Rafi and a scratching tool from Henri, she chose a section of great flat antler of the giant deer that was pulled from the cave, and sat down to carve into it a picture such as she and Doh Brom had shared when they sat alone in the evening, filling the scratches in with ink. When she was done, she lugged it up the bluff trail again, and left it as a signpost at the end of the travois drag. It was a very long and convoluted attempt at chronicling their adventure, but at the end, two female warriors stood side by side, a bear's head behind the taller one with the spear; a great spotted cat's face over the other, who bore two blades. Somehow, she hoped Doh Brom would see it, and understand what was meant. She tied the rawhide lanyard with the extra cat tooth that Henri had presented her with as a token of their unspoken camaraderie.

The final day was spent taking on fresh water for the journey, filled from the cave with the spring. They were low on food, but that could be made up once they were back in friendly waters. The longer boat rowed by four men took their water barrels back aboard. With a last look back, Sinbad, Tishimi, and Henri climbed aboard the smaller vessel and Ralf pushed them into the icy surf before clambering aboard all wet and full of grins. He was smiling again, because his ribs felt much better. His blonde hair and beard sparkled in the late afternoon sunshine as he took up his own oar and began to row with more vigor than he'd had in days.

"You seem in a good mood," Henri said sourly as he bent unhappily to his own oar. He'd be glad to be back aboard, where the sailors did all the work. Why Sinbad had insisted that they remained behind until the end was a mystery to him.

Ralf chuckled. "That's because I actually enjoy a little hard work. You should try it, maybe build up some of those scrawny muscles," he shot back. "The ladies love a brawny man!"

Henri snorted. "The only muscle I intend on using once we are in port is sadly in need of an intense workout or three. The rest of me is fine—or so I have been told. Unfortunately, that will have to wait for now. Besides, what most women desire is a man with wit and charm."

"Bah," the Viking shot back, "The women you attract just want to be paid. Give them enough coin and they will tell you anything you want to hear."

"Not all of them," Henri insisted, recalling Myeega; who had proved most ardent for a woman with an infant at the breast. Still, he took no real offense, for this was a game he and Ralf played to wile away the time, and they both knew it annoyed Tishimi. So they bickered openly about their personal lovemaking knowledge and prowess all the way to the ship.

Across from Ralf, Sinbad smiled as well, but while he rowed, his mind was already planning the next adventure. He was very grateful for the treasure they had taken aboard, which made their journey to the land of fire and ice well worth the effort it had taken and all the dangers they had been in. Only one life lost this time, and that of a fool and complaining laggard that no one aboard had liked. The crew could not complain too much, for they would be rewarded well. And there was little chance that anyone else would find this place, for Rafi had confided privately as he examined Sinbad's wounds that he did not feel they were in the same time as their own. Lesser men would have been unnerved by that, but Sinbad had seen many wondrous things in his career, and so he shrugged it off as the best possible way to protect the exact location of their bounty.

Tishimi sat opposite of Henri, and though the long oar was unwieldy for her, she didn't complain. In fact, she was very quiet, her back to the land of fire and ice they were leaving, but her mind split between the things she had learned about herself there, and the imminent return to adventuring she knew would come once Sinbad sold his cargo. Looking up, she realized they were close to the Blue Nymph now, the familiar ship riding low in the water with her hold full of ivory. The longer of the two auxiliary boats was empty with oars stowed, and it was being drawn up by bow and stern lines attached to pulleys on the spar. Soon she would be back on that deck, and this evening would have a good night's sleep in the hammock in her own tiny little quarters. It was as close to a home as she had ever had since she left her family's dwelling in flames years ago.

So many roads I could have taken, but this became my destiny. I must content myself with that and not question fate, she decided, and from that point forward, she let the ghosts of the past remain in the land of the dead.

They set sail the next morning at dawn, after the crew was assembled on deck and Saeed's blade was consecrated to the sea, forever to rest near the land where he died. Sinbad was up and down the deck after that, seeing to his ship, flitting from one end to the other as if he had never been injured. Being back on board his beloved Blue Nymph did wonders for his health and spirits. In fact, it was he who sang them into and out of the fog, and soon they found themselves back into far more familiar and warmer waters. His crew cheered their captain, and he beamed, but sent them back to work, for he was eager to sell what he had brought out of the land of fire and ice, and then arrange for his next voyage.

The lion skins they would take to a professional tannery and have them made into silk lined rugs. There were four for the companions, and the fifth of them was almost in two pieces, so he decided to split that one between Omar and Rafi, who had kept his crew safe and his ship intact by their unusual cooperation. He had heard the story of the attack of killer whales, and wanted to reward the two of them for their wisdom in trusting one another. Each would be given a half to remind them that working together under pressure was what made a team out of talented individuals. Perhaps a small bit could be made into something for Haroun as well, for the boy was most helpful. As a captain, he was truly blessed with such a dedicated crew.

Tishimi sat and meditated down on the foredeck. Ralf and Henri were already up too, and arguing about what brothel they should chose in the next port. Omar was haranguing his crew to pay attention to sails, and shouting up to Haroun to stop playing his infernal pipes. Rafi was likely somewhere below, examining the ivory and stretched skins before cataloging all he could write about them in some scroll.

Sinbad El Ari smiled into the salt spray, glad to be alive and well after such a wondrous journey. The stories that he would tell, he had no doubt would survive long after his body had returned to the water it was born to sail. Ah, but Allah was generous with His blessings, and life was satisfying to those who shrugged off danger, and seized each new dawn as part of one long and wondrous adventure.

THE END

FROZEN IN TIME

When my initial Sinbad story for Airship 27 appeared in the very first volume of SINBAD: THE NEW VOYAGES, I knew I'd be doing another one at some point. I have always the loved adventurous tales of the Middle-Eastern sailor, and the revamped concept as laid out by Ron Fortier really appealed to me. I had a blast writing that seminal piece, which flew from my fingers on the keys to become paragraphs on the page. I love when that happens! I had begun a story line with the introduction of some sort of magical navigation devices in that first installment, and I've been itching to make more use of it. Other projects with firm deadlines got in the way, as did things in my home life; but always, Sinbad was somewhere in the back of my mind, beckoning me to come on another voyage with him and his stalwart companions.

When I finally did sit down to work on the next adventure, I wanted to take our intrepid captain of the Blue Nymph, along with his comrades and crew, someplace that they would never normally go. Fantasy backdrops I am no stranger to, because they've become a regular feature of my writing, and many Sinbad stories of the past have featured mythical creatures and beings, and monsters galore. Yet there are plenty of fantastic-appearing settings within the actual history of our own world, and so it was just a matter of choosing some exotic place and time. The idea of making a rousing good tale is to challenge the characters by placing them in a foreign situation that is well beyond their imagining. Most of the regular cast are from a warm part of the world, so a frozen landscape filled with unprecedented dangers in climate, creatures, and other humans seemed the perfect antithesis. I started thinking about an ice age locale, and the giant megafauna creatures that populated the earth at the time would provide the monster element that is so important in Sinbad stories. From there on in, it was just a matter of figuring out what the purpose of the voyage was to be.

As a writer, you have to ask yourself a lot of questions about where this story is headed. When you're working on someone else's initial concept, it's important to honor the series continuity. If there is a common thread in all the Sinbad tales that have ever been told, it's the idea of finding riches in the midst of all that danger and intrigue. What in the world though would our enterprising captain find in a frigid wasteland that would be worth taking back to his own world? Thinking about the creatures he would encounter, it occurred to me that woolly mammoths had gigantic tusks, and I am sure that ivory was a lucrative trade item in Sinbad's time. So Sinbad now had something to covet in an unfamiliar landscape, and it was just a matter of wending my way through a plausible plot toward that inevitable victorious conclusion.

I don't just throw a story together that has any kind of historical backdrop. I do a lot of research, and this one was no different. First of all, I had to settle on a particular era and then an area, because the types of creatures and people that you would encounter varied depending on which part of the last ice age you were in and exactly where this was all taking place. For instance, one thing I found out is that the classic saber toothed cats were only found on the American continents, while most of the woolly mammoths and rhinos were Eurasian creatures. Neanderthal man had different hunting techniques than the Homo Sapiens of the time. Some animals we would recognize today lived in that frozen world. So I had to tailor my 'monsters' and my human guest stars to fit the scenes I had in mind, or risk putting someone or something in the wrong place. Not all my readers might know the difference, but I would, and it would bother me to take the easy route. I love a challenge anyway.

Part of research is looking at things you really wish you didn't have to know about. I spent a lot of time on the megafauna creatures, trying to get them just right. Not all of them were as huge as we picture, and fortunately some still have modern world contemporaries. I watched a bunch of Youtube videos on elephants, rhinos, and lions to understand how these creatures would move and interact with each other, and any humans who might be encountered. Hunting techniques and butchering skills were important to the story. One of the hardest scenes to write was the hunting of mammoths, so I had to watch an elephant being speared to death by multiple native hunters to do it correctly. It was short but brutal, and the knowledge was vital to the tale, so I forced myself to view it several times. I know more about mammoth hunting now than I ever expected to learn, and you can't help but admire our distant ancestors for surviving and thriving in such a harsh and demanding environment.

You have to be dedicated to what you are writing to make that kind of effort. I love what I do, and I really have enjoyed working within Sinbad's world. I hope that comes through in the stories I spin, and that you all enjoy reading them as much as I have writing them. I'm far from done with Sinbad yet!

NANCY HANSEN - An avid reader and prolific writer of fantasy and adventure fiction for over 30 years, Nancy A. Hansen is the author of many novels, anthologies, and short stories. You can find some of her work at **Pro Se Press** where she has a selection of original offerings of novel length under her imprint *HANSEN'S WAY*, as well as numerous short stories that have been contributed to various Pro Se multi-author publications. She also shares a children's adventure series called *Companion Dragons Tales* with co-authors Roger Stegman and Lee Houston Jr.

At Airship 27, Nancy has contributed short stories to *Sinbad-The New Voyages* and *Tales From The Hanging Monkey* anthologies, and she has an ongoing series of the very popular Jezebel Johnston pirate novels, including a 4 book omnibus. She also contributed to the Airship 27 anthology, *Legends of New Pulp Fiction.*

Nancy has also written for **Mechanoid Press** in their *Monster Earth* debut anthology, and at Flinch Books contributed to *Restless: An Anthology of Mummy Horror.* Nancy also has a story in the charity anthology *Lost Children,* which benefits groups that help abused and exploited youngsters.

Nancy has an Amazon Author Page at https://www.amazon.com/Nancy-Hansen/e/B009OGK632/ref=dp_byline_cont_ebooks_3

Her books are also available on Barnes & Noble online and some on Smashwords.

Nancy currently resides on an old farm in beautiful, rural eastern Connecticut with an eclectic cast of family members, and one very spoiled dog.

The Mages of the Obsidian Shard

By Greg Hatcher

Τhe black edifice carved out of the northern cliffs of the island loomed over the waves like a gargoyle made of dark glass. Though the sun beat mercilessly down on it in these tropical latitudes, the light barely penetrated its obsidian walls. Even as evening approached and the sun grew huge and red in the western sky, the light directly behind it merely caused the edges of the tower to glow faintly purple, the vaguely dizzying purple of the after-image of an explosion. It was difficult to look upon and had there been any human observers of the phenomenon they would doubtless have turned away.

There were no observers, though, not even gulls. All avoided the island of the Mages. It had been so since before the earliest sailors made their crude maps and it was so today. Doubtless it would remain so as long as the tower of black glass stood watch over the western seas. The edifice reeked of sorcery and evil; it had once been said that the tower was forged with the dark magics of the molten rivers that flowed through Hell itself, summoned to the surface and frozen into the tower's current shape to serve the needs of the wizards that dwelt there.

But these things were said no more— the Mages had made a concerted effort to eradicate the memory of their order from human histories. Like most magic, their works were best served with darkness and secrecy. Only the most erudite historians even knew that there had ever been an Order of the Obsidian Shard, let alone that it was still active today. And those few greybeards that knew the name tended to think of it as myth.

However, the Order was no myth, as Sinbad El Ari was soon to discover. A gathering was taking place in the tower of black glass that would have dire consequences for his life and the lives of his crew.

Five figures in black silken robes stood in a chamber in the top floor of the black tower. Each robe bore a bizarre scarlet crest on its back, a broken crescent pierced with a diamond-shaped blade.

"Seven years," intoned the robed figure at the head of the stone slab that served as a table in the council chamber. "Seven years and we must replenish the Shard. Have we a candidate?"

"A mighty warrior is called for," a second one said. "The Shard's requirements are strict. 'A man with the strength of ten. A man whose sword has claimed many lives. A man who has shown nobility and compassion. A man upon whom the gods smile.' We have gazed into the crystal and we have found such a man."

"Can there be more than one candidate?" A third asked, hesitation in the voice. "What if there is a problem? An obstacle? Perhaps our warrior will not—"

"What care we for the wishes of mortal men?" the first robed one cut in. "We care only for our lives and the life of the Shard. We must be restored. And so the Shard must be replenished. Bring the warrior to us. You know what happens if you do not."

There was a muttered assent from the group. The third figure, the one who had raised the objection, was silent.

"Where is the man now?" the leader asked. "What does the crystal show?"

"He is at sea still," answered another. A gloved hand sketched a rune in the air over the slab. The air shimmered and revealed a picture of a calm blue sea. In the midst of this was a sailing ship with the figure of a nude mermaid carved into its prow. The sail was filled and there was the faint noise of waves splashing mingled with the chorus of an old sea chantey, as sailors went about their work.

"Closer," the leader said.

The picture zoomed in to reveal a brawny, bare-chested man leaning over the railing, staring out to sea. "They make for port," explained the one who had sketched the rune. "In Aghrapur. He is already halfway ours. We just need to nudge events a little and we will be poised and ready for him."

"It is pleasing to hear this." The leader nodded. "At the full of the moon, then. In five days' time. The warrior will be here, atop this very slab, and all will once again be well with us."

"Not so well with the warrior, though." No one could see which had spoken, and so the leader chose to ignore this impertinence, as well as the few mordant chuckles that followed.

Sinbad El Ari leaned back against the railing and sighed. He was on the foredeck of his vessel, the *Blue Nymph*, letting the fresh spray soothe his bare back as he watched his sailors go about their business in the afternoon heat. He could see that all was well, yet he was uneasy.

"Something ails this crew, Omar," he murmured to the man standing next to him at the rail. "Despite the fact that we will be in Aghrapur tomorrow with each of them looking at shore leave and a newly-fat purse once payment is made for the cargo, there is something amiss. I can feel it."

"Of course you can, my captain." Omar was Sinbad's first mate, a small burly man with a graying beard and a perpetually sour expression. However, his nut-brown face split in a small smile at his captain's dark musings. "A crew has moods just as the sea does. I should be surprised indeed if you could not sense them—however!" He raised a hand as Sinbad made to interrupt. "I also have been aware of this small unrest, and I assure you it is best to let the men sort it out among themselves. A good captain, and his mate, would do well to remain out of these things. Sometimes it is a light hand required at the tiller."

"Well, what is it, then?" Sinbad relaxed a little at Omar's words, but he did not let this show. He turned his scowl upon the mate. "Is the captain not even allowed to know the source of the discontent?"

"Ralf and Tishimi had words. I do not know the source of this disagreement exactly, but there was a quarrel that barely escaped an escalation to blows. Thanks be to the gods that it did not for there would most surely have been blood on the decks." Omar's brows knitted in distaste. "Truly, had I wished to administrate childish squabbles I should have stayed on land with my wives and children. Now the crew tiptoes about for fear of provoking a recurrence, and there are whispered arguments among them which of the two had the right of it. Of course Ralf and Tishimi do not speak at all, but stalk about the ship like angry cats."

"Oh, for—" Now Sinbad was merely exasperated. "Less than a day from shore leave and division of spoils? What manner of foolishness—"

"Children, as I said." Omar shrugged and spread his hands. "What can be done? Let it shake out on its own."

"No." Sinbad shook his head. He pulled his shirt from where it had been draped over the rail and tugged it on. "I'll have the truth of this out of them. They are my fiercest warriors. If they cannot get along then our battle readiness is compromised. Either this is worked out or one of them is off the ship."

"You would kick over the hornet's nest, then?" Omar looked nonplussed. "Would it not be better—"

"It would not." Sinbad, his expression a roiling thundercloud of annoyance, strode to the ladderway without waiting to hear the rest of it.

Omar watched him go and muttered under his breath, "Children. Allah has cursed me with a shipload of children."

Despite his annoyance, Sinbad knew that this was a matter to be handled delicately. So he decided to start with Tishimi, for two reasons: the first being that, despite being the only female on the ship, the Asian warrior's daughter was far more likely to give him a dispassionate recounting of the incident. The other was privacy. Because Tishimi was a woman, she was the only crewmember aboard the *Blue Nymph* other than Sinbad himself accorded the luxury of her own cabin.

Sinbad rarely visited Tishimi in her quarters. The woman was so fiercely private that it seemed a violation, and it might have set tongues to wagging; though, Sinbad reflected, gossip was an inevitable consequence of an active crew at sea, and the truth of it was that he had no more control of it than he did over the winds that propelled his vessel across the waves. Nevertheless, he was resolved that he would put a stop to this particular— what? He was not even sure. Well, he would have it out of Tishimi, whatever it was.

He rapped on the oaken door and heard Tishimi's voice telling him to enter.

He had not been down here in weeks and was surprised to see the alterations the samurai woman had made. It was a tiny berth created by putting a wall up at the rear of the oarsmen's rows of benches below decks; originally a hasty improvisation using found lumber and driftwood, but over the years Tishimi had crafted it into a miniature shrine to her homeland with walls of split bamboo, an oaken door scavenged from a wreck the *Blue Nymph* had come across in a recent foray to the northern seas, and a couple of small wall hangings. There were also wall mounts for her weapons, and a chest for her clothing and other meager possessions that, with a folded blanket on top, also served as a place for her to sit with a tablet on her lap to practice her calligraphy. This was where she sat now, though the tablet lay propped against the bulkhead. Her sleeping accommodations were a simple straw mat that she rolled up during the day. In the rear of the room was a round glass porthole set into the bulkhead, another salvage piece that Ralf and Omar had helped her to install some months ago.

Sinbad nodded at it. "That's a fine piece of work," he said. "You certainly coaxed a level of craft out of the lads we don't usually see them display at sea."

Tishimi glanced at the porthole and for a moment allowed a flicker of satisfaction to cross her normally expressionless face. "Ralf and Omar only did the cutting on the bulkhead. The fitting and the glass work is mine; my father worked metal all his life and though his specialty was swords, shipwrights occasionally asked him to assist with their metal fittings. Rails, portholes, and the like. The polish is an old formula of my family's, the same I use on my blades." She turned to face her captain. "But you are not here to discuss my cabin."

"No." Sinbad decided to get right to it. "I want to know who is leaving my ship, you or Ralf."

He had thought to shock her, to shake her usually rigid code against displaying emotion. But her answer shocked him instead. "It was Ralf leaving that provoked our quarrel," she said, surprised. "I told him it was a traitor's act to put his needs in front of those of his shipmates. We sail in dangerous waters. For him to just *go*, without any thought for—"

Sinbad held up a hand. "Wait. How is it—perhaps you should begin at the beginning. What is this about Ralf leaving the ship? I know nothing of this."

"Exactly!" Tishimi's brow furrowed with anger. "He is keeping secrets! The honorable thing would be to go first to his captain, the man to whom he has sworn his—"

"Tishimi. Hold, please." Sinbad could feel himself losing control of the conversation. Sometimes Tishimi's samurai worldview blinded her to the realities of living as part of a ship's crew. "First of all, Ralf is not a servant or a vassal. None of you are. The *Blue Nymph* is our home and our livelihood, yes, but each voyage is its own undertaking. No one on this ship is indentured to me. You do not pass judgement on Ralf's choices any more than any of your shipmates are allowed to pass judgement on your own. Your duty, your *oath*, is to support this crew at sea, in all dangers and contingencies. That is the way of it. Can you hold to that oath or will we be putting you ashore in Aghrapur as well?"

As Sinbad spoke, Tishimi's face had been by turns angry, then resigned, and now was faintly shamed. Sinbad pretended not to notice. Part of being a captain was leaving his crew their pride whenever possible. But he would hear it said out loud. "Well?"

"Yes, my captain." Tishimi's voice was barely above a whisper.

"Then we will speak no more of it." Sinbad turned to go.

"Will you at least speak to Ralf?" Tishimi sounded almost plaintive.

"Of course I will. It is, in fact, where I go now." Sinbad paused. "But why is this so important to you? If Ralf leaves, it is his affair. Surely, you and Ralf are not—I mean—"

"No!" Tishimi looked briefly horrified. "I have forsworn all such— that is—I do not wish to speak of my personal conduct in these matters, Captain," she finished, awkwardly. "Or anyone's, really. But Ralf—he is not himself, this woman has bewitched him."

Aha. There it is, at last. Suddenly Sinbad realized what was going on. "You are saying Ralf is leaving the ship for a woman? He intends to take a wife?"

"So he says," Tishimi said.

"Well." Sinbad shrugged. "I cannot begrudge him. It is the way of men and women the world over, Tishimi. She awaits him in Aghrapur?"

"Yes. But—" Tishimi shook her head. "Really, Captain, you must speak with him. You must know I do not begrudge him any happiness either, but this—it is not— it happens too suddenly. The woman— she is not *right* for Ralf. You will see."

"There's that judgement again." Sinbad put the hint of a whipcrack in it. Tishimi's eyes lowered, and he relented, adding with a laugh, "Well, anyway, I daresay this truth is lost on a warrior such as yourself, but the unlikeliness of love between any two people is also the way of the world, you know. I'll talk to him. It may just be a passing fancy that has resulted in an entanglement Ralf cannot escape, something that perhaps a prideful man such as Ralf might not admit to a woman. Man-to-man, and especially man-to-captain, may be something else. But on the other hand—" Sinbad spread his arms. "If a life ashore with a wife and family is truly what he wants, then our duty is to support him in this as well. We'll bid him farewell and wish him all the joy in the world, and then sail on. *That* is our oath as his shipmates. Remember it."

At last Tishimi nodded.

Sinbad closed the door and strode back toward the ladderway. Ralf taking a wife—had it been anyone but Tishimi saying it, he would not have believed it. Now it was curiosity, as much as the matter of his crew's morale, that sent Sinbad in search of the Norseman.

He found Ralf squatting on the aft deck, mending a line, while the crew parted around him as though he were a rock in the rapids. As Sinbad approached, the few others on the deck suddenly made it their business to be elsewhere, leaving just the two men.

Ralf grunted. "Captain." He started to rise.

Sinbad waved him to stay as he was. Instead, the lithe seaman dropped to his haunches opposite the giant Northlander. "So, I hear that you are to be congratulated."

Ralf looked startled, then his brow furrowed. "Tishimi should mind her own business."

"She minds ship's business, and she did right to speak of the matter to me." Sinbad raised an eyebrow. "I am wondering why you did not."

Ralf made a noise that was almost a growl. "I was going to," he said. "I just am not sure how best to— I am not sure. I was thinking on it."

"Tell me of the woman."

"We met six months gone, shortly before we set out from Aghrapur." Ralf's eyes softened. "In the market. Delacrois and the others were off to the tavern but I was tired of tavern meals and sought other food. I craved other fare, something different for my palate. Truthfully I longed for the food of my homeland—and suddenly, as if in answer to a wish, there was a stall with fruits and other goods from the north; and fresh, not dried such as one usually sees in these latitudes. I spent almost as much as I would on a night's debauchery." Ralf flushed a little. "I was as greedy as a child, but it was so good, Captain. And as I took the last of the apples, she approached and she looked so forlorn that I was shamed by my gluttony. I gave all I had left to her. Ariadne was her name. She was so moved by this that she invited me to dine with her and her father."

Sinbad was amused. "And to think, all these years I have wasted trying to win women with treasure and noble deeds."

"She said it was noble to give up something I so clearly wanted myself. What I had was two pears and an apple. So that is what I gave her."

"It clearly was enough."

"I almost did not go, I— Captain, I do not know how to explain it. I see you, and Delacrois—even Omar—you all know how to talk to a beautiful woman," Ralf blurted. "I have not the gift of words. I only knew that she was sad and I wanted to see her smile. I would have given anything. But I feared I would say or do something wrong and spoil what good she thought of me." He shook his head. "Then I remembered the dangers we have faced at sea and felt foolish. But still I feared. I was frozen. And then she—" Now Ralf's flush was beet red. "She laid a hand on my arm and said, 'It will be all right.' It was as though she could see right inside me, and she wanted to see me smile and be happy. As I just had with her. It was a powerful thing."

Sinbad thought of the women he had known, and the few he had truly loved. "Aye. It is indeed powerful. And rare."

Ralf straightened a little, almost as if waking from a dream. "Anyway, that is how we met. We had dinner in her father's house and I met him as well. He is a trader of sorts, not rich, but not poor. Ariadne and I spent most of the rest of the leave together, mostly walking the city and sometimes sitting in her father's garden. When it was time to go to sea again I knew I loved her and I promised to return, and that time to stay." He shrugged. "We are returning. So— there it is."

Sinbad nodded. "But why keep it a secret, Ralf? This is a joy to be shared. Did you think we would be angry? We are your shipmates—your friends. You are family to me, and to Omar and all the rest. We would be happy for you."

"There is the part I did not tell you." Ralf looked uncomfortable. "Her father is a trader—in magics. Sorcery. With the history of this vessel being what it is—well, I know sorcerers are not your favorite people. Nor mine, to be honest. But I think Ariadne's father is a good man. He gave me a small mirror, where I may look upon her and she upon me while I am at sea. That is what Tishimi saw. It was none of her business," he added fiercely. "And—well, we quarreled. Now she has tattled on me like a palace gossip. I meant no secrecy, and I am not a traitor. I was coming to you, Captain, but after Koura and the other wizards we have faced—it was— difficult, that's all. I was working up to it."

Sinbad held up a hand. "Ralf. No one doubts your heart. Not I, not anyone. Not even Tishimi. She but feared for you, and she did not mention the sorcery to me at all. You do her a disservice. But I admit I am a little bothered. We all have reason to be suspicious of wizardry." He stroked his trimmed beard and thought. "Still, she cannot help her lineage. You are sure of this girl? You love her? And she you?"

"Yes she does. And I do her, Captain." No hesitation. "I am certain of that. My indecision is mostly— I am not sure what I shall do ashore. I must find a way to provide for Ariadne and myself. As you may guess, I prefer not to join her father's business."

"Why, as to that—" Sinbad clapped the blond giant on his shoulder.

"The *Blue Nymph* always needs a broker for cargo. None of these Aghrapur merchants can be fully trusted, but I have trusted you with my very life. Who better than one of my own men to set up in business in the harbor here? And with my recommendation other captains will trust you as well. In no time at all you could be living in a house on the hill with your woman and your many fine sons, telling them tales of your days at sea. You could even still sail with us every once in a while." He grinned. "Lest you grow too fat and lazy."

Ralf nodded and smiled. "It is a fine offer, Sinbad, but—"

"But nothing! It is done!" Sinbad stood. "Rest your mind, Ralf. We take care of our own. We will welcome your woman into our family, and as to her father, well, there are worse things than wizards. I would see this magic glass, though."

Ralf stood and pulled a small gilt-framed mirror out of his sash. "Here, Captain. I keep it with me always."

"Ha! You are a man in love indeed." Sinbad leaned forward to get a better look. The golden frame was sculpted to look like a fat smiling Buddha with his arms curling around, holding the glass in the middle. The glass itself swirled with a smoky violet mist, and then cleared to reveal a young olive-skinned woman with a cascade of brunette hair that fell freely about her shoulders. She wore a green sari and a sea-blue scarf. She turned and waved at the two men looking into the glass, then executed a small curtsy at Sinbad.

"She sees us?" Sinbad said, startled.

"It is the magic," Ralf said. He nodded and smiled at the girl and mouthed, *Soon*. She laughed and blew him a kiss. Then the mists covered the glass again. Ralf looked up at Sinbad and smiled, still blushing a little. He tucked the mirror back into his sash. "It only grants a moment or so. Just enough so we can see each other, and remember our love."

"That is a wonder." Sinbad shook his head, and then smiled back at the northlander. "And so is she. We shall prepare a celebration when we dock in Aghrapur such as the world has never seen. I vow that even your mighty appetites will be satisfied. Ralf, you are blessed. The gods are smiling upon you. Be of good cheer."

And in a tower made of black glass facing that very same sea, a gathering of black-clad wizards smiled as well.

"She sees us?" Sinbad said.

Two days later, in Aghrapur, the celebration aboard the *Blue Nymph* was in full swing. Henri Delacrois had appointed himself master of ceremonies and as such the Gallic archer had outdone himself, Sinbad was forced to admit. The feast he had put together was such that the table ran almost the entire length of the main deck of the ship, and the revels had spilled out on to the dock and even to a couple of the neighboring vessels in the harbor. There were two tavern girls dancing along the rail, each pirouette taking them towards what surely must be a disastrous fall, yet somehow the fall never materialized. Their clothing remained ever at the edge of decency, though the swirling veils and scarves appeared so accident-prone that it seemed that at any moment one or both of them would be wearing nothing at all. The girls were long experienced at this game, of course, and smiled demurely as the crewmen hooted and raised tankards of ale in appreciation.

"And it is only mid-afternoon," Omar muttered. He and Sinbad were on the foredeck overlooking the festivities, leaning against the rail. "By nightfall this debauch will engulf the entire port."

Sinbad's face quirked in a wry smile. "Did you expect less of Henri? He never needs much of an excuse for debauchery. And Ralf deserves it. The crew deserves it. We had a difficult time of it in the islands."

"I know." Omar's nod was grudging. "I even agree. It just chafes me that we are losing the boy. He has been a good crewman for us."

"As often as you have been married, surely you would not gainsay him." Sinbad's expression was carefully bland, though inwardly he was smiling broadly. Omar's wives were the subject of much speculation aboard ship—and much teasing from his captain, the only man who dared such.

"Pfagh!" Omar grimaced and declined to take the bait. Instead, he asked, "Where is Tishimi? I thought you had persuaded her to accept Ralf's decision."

Sinbad pointed. "There. She awaits the bride-to-be and her father."

Tishimi was standing on the dock, a few feet from where the ramp led aboard the *Blue Nymph*. She was clad in what she considered civilian attire, which is to say she had only worn the leather chest plate over her usual black silks. Other than that she was wearing her usual harness with her three blades: the dagger, her short blade, and her father's katana that she was never without. She managed to remain aloof from the celebration taking place all around her. Though she too held a tankard of ale, it seemed to serve mostly as a prop. Her gaze was everywhere, surveying the entire tableau with the watchful eye of a hawk.

"Like a sentry," Omar observed. He raised an eyebrow. "You stationed her there, didn't you? You harbor doubts about this union of Ralf's as well."

Sinbad smiled. "I have always said—'Trust in Allah, but—' "

"—'but tie up your camel.' Yes, I know." Omar smiled in return. "But what do you expect? Surely not a battle. Tishimi is a warrior, not—"

"Her father's katana," Sinbad explained. "The soulsword is proof against ensorcelment. If Ralf is truly bewitched as Tishimi claims, she will know when the woman approaches. At which point she will quietly let me know and we will act accordingly. If, on the other hand, all is as it seems, why, the party will proceed with no one the wiser."

"It is well to be cautious." Omar nodded in approval.

"So it seemed to me this morning." Sinbad sighed. "I have to say, though, now that the party is in full swing and there is so much joy here, I feel a bit foolish—hold! Here they come. Soon we will have an answer."

Sinbad and Omar leaned forward a little to get a view of them as they approached. Ralf was waving and shaking hands with enthusiastic celebrants, many of whom Sinbad was sure had never met the Norseman, but just locals who were swept up in the mood of the occasion. Ariadne was as beautiful as she had appeared in the glass, smiling somewhat dazedly at the crowd, but obviously delighted to be on Ralf's arm. Behind them came a plump older man with a white beard and a turban laced with golden thread, looking somewhat worn but nevertheless regal. He too was smiling and shaking hands with various partygoers as they approached the gangplank.

Sinbad could not help but smile at the picture the three of them presented; he felt absurdly fatherly all of a sudden. But he did not forget Tishimi and her mission, and he watched her carefully as Ralf and Ariadne came up to her. He could see Tishimi lean forward, and then she smiled and embraced the girl. At that Ralf's own smile, already broad, now seemed as if it would split his entire face. He gathered both women to him and hugged them mightily.

Sinbad could hear Omar make a noise that was somewhere between a snort and a laugh. "Now, truly, I have beheld miracles."

"It is the clearest signal we could have been given," Sinbad said. "The girl's heart is true. Tishimi would never have allowed such a thing otherwise." He realized that his back muscles were unclenching for the first time since he had arisen that morning. "We may as well go and enjoy the party."

Omar held up a hand. "Captain, first you must let Ralf present his betrothed to you. It is the way of his people. You are the closest he has to a chieftain."

Sinbad sighed. "Captain's burden. Very well, then. You should at least go and make sure there is some of the wine left. The *good* wine, I mean, before Henri drains it all. We must have some to toast the happy couple."

Omar bobbed his head in acknowledgment and disappeared into the crowd, just as Ralf and Ariadne emerged. "Captain Sinbad!" the Northerner said, somewhat hoarsely. "Allow me to present my woman, soon to be my wife. Ariadne, this is my master, Captain Sinbad."

"Not for much longer," Sinbad said, with a smooth bow. "You are taking him from me, my lady. But I console myself with the thought that you will bring him much happiness."

"As he brings me," Ariadne said. Her voice was soft and shy.

She is terrified, Sinbad realized. *The girl must know of the strife aboard ship.* He leaned forward and took her hand. "I am but jesting," he said, putting reassurance into his tone. "Please know that we of the *Blue Nymph* wish nothing but the best for you and for Ralf. I have no sons of my own but this lad is as close to me as one, and gives me as much pride. So these nuptials, then, will make you my daughter. You must think of me and this crew as family."

Ralf beamed at this. "Did I not tell you?"

Ariadne smiled and would have spoken, but the bustle of her father pushing forward prevented this. "Captain Sinbad. It is truly a pleasure to meet you at last. I am Balthazar, the father of the bride-to-be." He thrust out a hand and Sinbad grasped it briefly. The merchant's grip was dry and firm.

"Welcome aboard the *Blue Nymph*." Sinbad waved a hand at the feast table. "Please enjoy our hospitality. Before Henri and Ralf devour it all," he added with a laugh.

"He jests," Ralf put in, embarrassed. "Truly, Captain, I am too excited to eat. I can hardly—" His voice trailed off as a shadow fell over the ship. He looked up.

So did Sinbad. He sucked in his breath sharply and swore.

Four giant winged lizards were in the sky above, circling the harbor. One let out an unearthly cry and dived toward the *Blue Nymph*. Sinbad could hear the revelers start to scream. He ignored this and leaped to the rail. "Tishimi! Henri! To me! Archers, weapons free! *Now*, Allah curse you! We are attacked!"

Ralf shoved Ariadne to the deck and moved between her and the beast that had apparently targeted them. "A sword! Anything!" he roared.

Someone threw him a belaying pin and he whirled it before him like a club. "You will regret this," he snarled at the approaching reptile. "Come then and meet your maker."

Sinbad turned to see Henri Delacrois and Tishimi Osara vault over the rail from the dock, ignoring the gangplank. Henri had his bow out and loosed a flurry of arrows at the creature. Now it was close enough that Sinbad could see the dragon-thing had a rider, a bald man in a black robe. "Henri! Not the beast! Its master! Put an arrow through him!"

Henri let fly with another barrage. The robed man merely laughed and waved, and Henri's arrows dropped to the deck, shimmered, and suddenly where there had been arrows there were now bright green vipers hissing and coiling towards Sinbad and the others. Tishimi Osara snarled something in her native tongue and slashed with her katana, and the vipers were gone, leaving only splintered arrows again. She was up to the foredeck in a bound, where she and Ralf stood shoulder-to-shoulder, in front of Sinbad and Ariadne and her father. "It seems we shall share one last battle together, my friend," she said to Ralf.

Ralf grunted in acknowledgement but said no more, as the lizard bore its rider to a few feet above where they stood. The party made ready to engage the beast but it halted in mid-air, the robed wizard pulling it up short as one would a horse, and its claws grasped Ralf by the shoulders and bore him away almost before the others could react. All save Tishimi Osara, who leaped forward and swung her katana in a mighty arc that should have severed the beast's leg and dropped Ralf safely to the deck. Instead, it bounced off and it was Tishimi herself that fell, cracking her head on the oaken rail. She collapsed in a heap.

"How—?" *Her sword is proof against all magics—can the beast be natural?* Sinbad's train of thought was cut off by a man's scream. This time it was Ariadne's father, who also was being hauled bodily into the sky by another of the dragon-beasts. This apparently completed their mission, for at a signal from the robed sorcerer astride the largest one, all four were off to the sky again, receding towards the horizon with a speed Sinbad had never seen before.

Taking Ralf and Balthazar with them.

Sinbad noted the direction with a seaman's eye. Straight west, towards— what lay that way? No land that he knew of.

He whirled to where Ariadne was sobbing on the deck. "Girl, what do you know of this? Who was that?" She was weeping so that Sinbad could hardly make sense of her words. He knelt beside her and grasped her shoulder. "Please. I must know what you know. We will go after them."

"The Mages," Ariadne could barely speak, her body shaking with sobs. "The Obsidian Isle. My father—Ralf— oh, Allah have mercy!" She tried to sit up. "My father and my love are both dead men!"

"Not while I have this ship and this crew. The promise I made? Here is where you see it fulfilled, daughter." Sinbad rose and faced the dock. "Omar! Gather our people!" he shouted. "We make sail within the hour!" He turned and surveyed his vessel, and only then did he register the unconscious form of Tishimi Osara, lying crumpled in a heap where she had fallen. To his horror he saw a small trickle of blood pooling near where her head lay on the deck. He muttered another curse under his breath, then roared, "Someone find Rafi, his healing arts are needed here! Tishimi has fallen!" even as he moved to her side. Carefully he examined her—she was unconscious but breathing. *Ralf gone and Tishimi down,* he thought. *Our two best fighters. Still, we are not toothless yet.*

Rafi, the old scholar who served as the *Blue Nymph*'s medical officer when they were at sea, was pushing forward through the crowd. Sinbad waved him to the foredeck and pointed. "Help her," he said, then strode over to the ladderway. "Haroun! Henri! Clear this deck! The holiday is over! We have work to do!"

Haroun, still a little fuddled from wine, shook his head. "But the feast—" He looked at the table on the deck, still loaded with food. "What can we—"

"Store what can be stored." This was Omar, back on duty and all business now. "The fruits and meats will serve us well for the next few days, they can go below. When we are provisioned, give the rest to the crowd on the dock. Now!" he added. He turned to Sinbad. "I have this in hand, captain. See to the woman. And I think Rafi is wanting a word."

Sinbad nodded and turned back to where Rafi knelt over Tishimi. "She will live," the older man told Sinbad, his expression grim. "But I cannot rouse her. We must get her below. She needs rest and quiet."

"My cabin," Sinbad said. "Put her in my bed. I will make do elsewhere." For once, he reflected, Tishimi would sleep on something finer than a straw mat on the deck. "Until she wakes, at least." His teeth flashed in a brief grin. "If she takes issue with it then, we will know she is well."

"Aye." Rafi gestured for a couple of crewmen to help him and together, very carefully, they hoisted Tishimi's unconscious body to their shoulders and carried her to the ladderway, where other crewmen were waiting to lift her down off the foredeck. Once they had her down on the main deck, Rafi bawled for the rest of the crew embarked on cleanup to make a hole, and the men bore her body to the entrance to the captain's cabin.

Sinbad left them to it and turned to the girl Ariadne, who was no longer weeping, but stood staring blindly out to sea at the edge of the foredeck. "They took Ralf," she murmured in disbelief. "There was no reason."

Sinbad took her by the shoulders. "My lady," he said. "I beg you, do not give in to grief. We are mounting a rescue attempt right now; Omar will have us ready to cast off in minutes. We will return Ralf and your father to you. But I must know what you know," he repeated. "Who was that wizard? Why does he want them?"

Ariadne gazed back at him, uncomprehending. Then she seemed to gather herself. She squared her jaw and looked back at Sinbad with new purpose. "Yes," she said softly. "I believe you can save them. I will tell you everything, Captain. But for now you must make sail for the west. Straight into the setting sun. If you have charts I can show you."

Sinbad nodded, glad she seemed to be finding some strength of will again. "It can be done. Omar!" he bellowed, turning to the main deck. He noted with grim pleasure that under Omar's direction there was almost no sign left of the festivities, and he guessed they could be casting off even sooner than he had hoped. "Get us underway and then join us in my cabin."

In Sinbad's cabin, the most luxurious berth aboard the *Blue Nymph*, the captain stood with Omar, Rafi, and Ariadne looking over Sinbad's charts of the western sea. Behind them, Tishimi was lying in Sinbad's bunk, her head propped up upon silks and pillows, still unconscious.

"The Obsidian Mages?" Rafi blinked in surprise. "But that order is long gone. The glass island is a myth."

"We thought the same of Lemuria," Sinbad reminded him. "Until Koura."

Rafi nodded, reluctantly. "Even so— if what this girl says is true, we are defeated before we start. Look here." He reached under the chart table and unrolled an ancient and cracking scroll, ignoring the dust that billowed up from its edges. "This is the only information I have on the Obsidian Isle; a brief note in this scroll I discovered during my exploration of the ruins of the Lemurian palace. This crude drawing here and these warnings." He pointed to a rendering in black ink with red highlights of a sinister black tower in an open sea, with dragons circling in the sky.

"The beasts we saw," Omar said. "Impervious even to Tishimi's blade."

"Yes." Rafi nodded. "But there is more." He indicated lines of handwritten scarlet script next to the drawing. "The language is Atlantean. I am not as fluent as I would like but its rough approximation is, *All who approach the Island of the Magicians shall lose their lives and souls to the Tower of Black Glass. To climb the tower is to surrender all.* Not promising."

"Not exactly." This was Ariadne. She flushed a little as everyone looked at her. "It is not seemly for a woman to be a scholar of such things, I know," she went on. "But I did grow up assisting my father Balthazar and I learned things. You are mistranslating—it says the lives will be *taken* by the Tower. The difference is a small one but it reveals the reason why the Mages took Ralf and my father."

"And that is?" Rafi looked a little annoyed at being corrected by a girl barely into adulthood but Sinbad waved him to silence.

Ariadne took no notice of Rafi's irritation, or pretended not to. "The Mages are immortal," she explained. "They were the first taken by the Tower—it is a natural formation, born of an ancient breach between our world and the Underworld that lies beneath ours. Those early sorcerers went there in search of power a thousand years ago, but they learned that power comes at a price. The darkness must feed. It takes human lives. Thus threatened, those five wizards used their arts to achieve a compromise. They gained the use of the Underworld's energies and prolonged their own lives indefinitely, but they must continue to feed the hardened obsidian remnant, the Shard of Hell, that is all that remains of the breach. It is at the top of the Tower, protected by both sorcerous wards and by the dragon creatures, themselves remnants of an earlier era. The winged monsters have been granted a sort of immortality just from the presence of the Shard, as well."

"But why Ralf?" Sinbad pressed. "Your father—he at least is a wizard himself, but the Norseman—"

Ariadne looked as if she might start weeping again. "I am to blame," she said at last. "I spoke to my father of Ralf's adventures, and of this vessel. I was boasting of my love. But somehow Balthazar must have let slip these tales to the Mages. I think he might have—I do not know, but the Mages require the mightiest warrior in the lands to feed the Shard, a man of great strength and virtue. I think Balthazar might have perhaps inadvertently made them aware—I fear the worst, but I only know that Ralf is nearly their ideal candidate. The Shard must feed every seven years. At the full of the moon."

Sinbad chose to ignore the implications of betrayal on the part of the girl's father. *She cannot help her lineage,* he reminded himself. He said, "Very well. So we must devise a means to defeat the dragons and ascend the Tower. Omar, Rafi, let us think on this. I have an idea, but we must consult with some of the crew."

"I will stay and keep watch over your fallen warrior," Ariadne said softly. "It is the least I can do."

"As you wish. Omar, have the men set up another bunk in here, or at least sleeping silks and furs." Sinbad beckoned the others to join him. Exiting the cabin, the three men ascended to the foredeck. Sinbad turned to face the other two. "Well, Rafi? You are the closest we have to an expert. Is the girl telling the truth?"

Rafi nodded. "I believe so. And—" He hesitated. "I am not entirely sure of this, but we had her within a few feet of Tishimi's soulsword. Surely in the presence of deceit or dark magics, there would have been some sign."

Omar grunted. "Captain, I think the larger problem is defeating these flying reptiles. Wizardry I leave to our learned greybeard Rafi, but those things will have us sunk before we ever get close enough to shore for these Mages to notice us. Not to mention the impossibility of climbing a cliff of demon glass."

Sinbad grinned. "As to that, well, I think I may have a solution to both problems," he said. "We have two days yet before the full moon and so we need to set to work. Here is my plan..."

Below, in Sinbad's cabin, Tishimi Osara stirred and moaned. Ariadne was at her side in an instant. She laid a hand across the Asian woman's forehead and whispered, "Softly, now. You are injured."

"Must—" Tishimi struggled to sit up. "My place is—"

"Your place is here." Ariadne smiled. "Your captain orders it. We are already underway to rescue Ralf and my father."

Tishimi fell back, satisfied. Her eyes flickered up to meet Ariadne's steady gaze. "Do you know what those things were? Why the wizard set them on us?"

"I cannot say." Ariadne's eyes fell.

Tishimi struggled to one elbow. Her face was ashen with pain but there was no indication of it in her voice. "You cannot say— but you know, don't you? You recognized the sorcerer leading the attack."

"Please." Ariadne would not meet Tishimi's eyes. "There will be time later. You must rest and recover."

"Do not presume to tell me what I 'must' do, girl. I must protect this vessel. You know something that will help." Almost involuntarily, Tishimi glanced over at where her unsheathed soulsword was propped against the chart table. She sucked in her breath sharply. "You have not been honest with us," she whispered, then opened her mouth to shout.

But the shout never came. Ariadne sketched a runic gesture in the air and said simply, "Sleep now." Instantly Tishimi's eyes closed and she fell back into the silks.

Ariadne sighed. She stood and saw the naked blade leaning on the table. She made a sour face and picked up the scabbard from the pile of discarded clothing near the bunk and sheathed the katana. At her touch, the hilt glowed red, very slightly. "Sloppy," she muttered. She set the blade back against the table and then, thinking better of it, brought it over near the bunk and shoved it under the pile of leathers that Tishimi had been wearing before Rafi and the others had put her to bed.

She needs to sleep anyway, Ariadne thought. *She needs to heal. It is better thus. By the time she wakes—it will be too late.*

The next day and a half at sea passed without incident. The *Blue Nymph* had fair winds, speeding them towards the west with an ease that both pleased and worried Captain Sinbad. He spent a great deal of time conferring with the Gallic archer Henri Delacrois and he in turn had set all the crew that could be spared to work with sailcloth and ropes, rigging the weapons that Captain Sinbad hoped would be their salvation against the flying lizards guarding the Obsidian Isle. Meanwhile, Omar and Sinbad's other northern expatriate, William Byrne, spent a fair amount of time conferring about the longboats. The *Blue Nymph* only had two, and Omar was sure this was inadequate to the task.

"Captain, it's foolishness," Omar said flatly on the afternoon of the second day at sea. "As it is the crew is going to be severely strained—we are not a naval vessel, we are not ready for full and open warfare. We have won skirmishes in the past by being sly, we have struck from stealth and retreated, but this—faugh!"

"Sleep now."

Byrne nodded. "I confess, Captain, I find myself in agreement with Omar. Although I take your point that the creatures are natural and thus can be slain by natural means, I am not entirely sure we have the means at hand. Even with harpoons—"

"Never mind the harpoons," Omar put in. "We no longer have Ralf and I doubt any man left aboard can cast half as far as he. This leaves us Henri and his arrows, which have already proven ineffective. Worse, we shall only have the use of one of the boats, unless you plan to swim for shore."

"Ah, but we shall not be using the boats." Sinbad's eyes twinkled. "Nor shall we swim. Here, follow me." He gestured for them to follow him to the foredeck. They ascended the ladderway to see Rafi and Ariadne seated there, lotus-style, with a heavy five-foot by eight-foot tapestry spread out between them on the wooden deck.

Omar blinked. "Was that not a gift from the vizier?"

"Needs must," Sinbad said. He turned to Rafi. "Very well, let us see this miracle."

"Hardly more than a cantrip," Rafi admitted. "Still, it is very clever, and Ariadne knew of refinements that make it much easier and safer." He smiled at the girl, who in turn flushed a little but nevertheless looked pleased at Rafi's praise. "Go ahead. Show him."

Ariadne nodded and laid a hand on the maroon fabric. She said simply, "Rise."

The tapestry floated up off the planks, staying flat and level. Ariadne let her hand ride up with it until it was level with her eyes. She said, "Wait."

The tapestry stopped and hung in mid-air between Rafi and Ariadne, about four feet from the deck. Ariadne dropped her hand to her lap and smiled at the men, who were all open-mouthed in astonishment. Even Sinbad, and he had known it was coming. But to see such a thing!

"Name of the gods!" Omar blurted. "This— this is—"

"A flying carpet is a fairly common request for a merchant dealing in magics," Ariadne said modestly. "My father did two or three of them a month. Our first was created for Prince Husain of the Indies." She smiled. "Climb on."

"You first." Omar's face was screwed into a scowl of distrust, but whether it was aimed at the girl or the carpet itself, Sinbad could not determine. The captain could not entirely blame his second-in-command for being suspicious; Sinbad felt a little nervous about it himself.

"I will try it," Byrne said suddenly, his eyes bright. Sinbad hid a smile. Of all his crew, it was William Byrne who always was first to embrace new things. It was the man's restless wanderlust and desire for new horizons that had led him to joining the crew of the *Blue Nymph* in the first place. The Scottish explorer swung a leg up on to the floating tapestry as though he were mounting a horse and then grasped the edge of the fabric with his hand and hoisted himself up. Slowly he stood up, then walked from one end to the other. "By God, it really *is* a carpet," he said. "It is as flat and solid as though it had a floor beneath it."

"That was Ariadne," Rafi admitted. "I could levitate the thing but it was soft as a hammock. It was she who showed me her father's spells that allow it to remain flat and also to respond to voice command."

Sinbad nodded. "Well done," he said to Rafi. "To you both," he added, turning to Ariadne, who blushed. Then, grinning, he faced Byrne. "Off with you, William, I would test the thing myself." Byrne obediently hopped back to the deck of the *Blue Nymph* and Sinbad in turn clambered atop the floating carpet. For a moment he just stood there, frowning. He turned to Rafi. "And it responds to my voice? Only mine?"

"You must be touching it," Rafi said. "It is bound to its rider."

Sinbad nodded, again. He said, "Take me up."

The carpet rose with him, easily and steadily, and despite the wind at his back that filled the sails of the *Blue Nymph* he was not shaken or jostled. A smile of sheer joy lit his face. Soaring above the waves on this magic carpet—even at the tiller of his ship with a strong wind behind and fair seas ahead, he had never felt so free. If only their errand was not such a grim one.

At the thought he sobered. This was work. They had much to do. He said, "Point us in the direction of the Obsidian Isle."

The carpet adjusted slightly, turning just a little to starboard. The carpet was now more or less on the same heading as the *Blue Nymph*, westward into the afternoon sun. *The winds and weather are with us,* Sinbad thought. *Praise Allah for that. We have few enough advantages.* He said, "Higher."

The carpet obediently rose another two hundred feet. Now the ship below looked like a child's toy in a bath. Sinbad scanned the western horizon. Open seas still—no, wait! A tiny black lump, hardly more than a dot, several leagues west and a little north of their position, rose from the waves. Smaller black shapes circled in the air above. Suddenly one halted and then the others fell into line behind. Then they began to move towards where Sinbad floated in the sky. As they approached, Sinbad could discern wings flapping, even at a distance of what had to be three or four leagues. He muttered a curse, then added, "Return me to the ship."

The carpet moved gently but with great speed back to the deck of the *Blue Nymph*. Sinbad waved the men to silence as they all crowded around him, exclaiming with wonder. "We have no time," he said. "I was seen. The beasts are coming. All of you, to your posts! As we practiced, Omar, see to Henri and his archers, make sure we have the lines laid out and the braziers ready. And ready the longboats."

Omar nodded and scurried down the ladderway, bawling for Delacrois. Sinbad turned to Ariadne. "How many will this carry?"

"As many as can stand safely upon it," she said. "It is not a beast, it will not tire."

"Good. But I think the fewer of us, the better our chances. Stealth must be our aim. We will use the dragons as a distraction. William, you will accompany me— and—" He paused. They might need Rafi's arcane knowledge, but the crew would need his medical knowledge more if anyone was wounded. Well, the only way to trust the girl was to trust her, and he knew her heart was true. "Ariadne, you will come as well. No, old friend," he added as Rafi started to protest. "Omar will need you here. And Tishimi will need care as well. Once we free Ralf he is worth five warriors at least," he finished with a smile and clapped Rafi on the shoulder. "Be of good cheer. This is not the worst we have faced."

"It's no garden of houris, either," Rafi grumbled, but did not argue further.

Sinbad nodded and turned to the rail looking out over the main deck. He roared, "The casks! We need them up here, now! At least six of them! Hurry!"

In all the bustle of preparation, no one saw Ariadne quietly descend the ladderway and enter Sinbad's cabin, where Tishimi Osara slept on. Her sleep was uneasy, her forehead slick with sweat. She moaned as Ariadne approached.

The merchant's daughter looked annoyed and a little sad. "Not yet, valiant one," she said. She waved a hand over the Asian woman's face and murmured a phrase. The frown smoothed out and Tishimi's breathing softened and became more regular.

Ariadne smiled a little in return, but it was rueful. "You are brave and good," she said softly. "You are fighting me. You must not, my sister. This is for Ralf. I dare not deepen your sleep any more. Just—just *stop* it," she finished awkwardly. Her face was a mask of helplessness and frustration. "You must not wake. You cannot tell them. You will ruin everything if you do."

Tishimi moaned again. Ariadne ignored it and left the cabin, closing the door firmly behind her.

The longboats were in the water now, each with a crew of eight; four at the oars and three each armed with bow and arrows, and one tending a charcoal brazier that Delacrois had set up in the stern of each. Delacrois commanded one, and Haroun was in charge of the other.

Omar was at the tiller of the *Blue Nymph*; for something this tricky, Sinbad trusted no one else, other than himself. But he was needed elsewhere. He and William Byrne heaved the last of the casks on to the enchanted carpet, and then Sinbad buckled on the leather belt that held his scimitar in a long scabbard. Byrne carried a longsword in a sling on his back and a dagger in his belt. Sinbad suddenly noticed Ariadne was no longer there. "Where is..?"

"Here, Captain." Ariadne was ascending the ladderway. Sinbad saw that she had changed to a simple blouse and breeks, with a sash wrapped around her middle that held a dagger in its sheath. She had also exchanged her sandals for boots of soft leather. "I thought I should have more practical attire."

Sinbad nodded. "Good. Climb on." She did so, and Sinbad looked at the carpet at his feet and said, "Rise."

The carpet lifted to a point some fifty feet above the crow's nest of the *Blue Nymph*. Sinbad eyed the approaching dragons, certainly only a half-league's distance by now, and said to Ariadne, "How fast is this thing? How maneuverable?"

Ariadne's teeth flashed briefly in a nervous grin. "It depends what you wish for, Captain. You must be careful in your phrasing; the magic does only what you say, not what you think."

Sinbad nodded. It was typical of enchantments, he thought. Very well, he would be specific. He looked down at the carpet and said, "Fly us to the dragons, maneuver us as closely as you can but keep us safely clear of their claws and jaws. Weave us rapidly between them in circles but do not spill us off into the sea below."

Instantly the carpet was in motion, smooth and fast. Ariadne nodded at Sinbad in approval.

Sinbad gestured to the casks. "Loosen the lids, William. We shall have to be quick."

Byrne pulled his dagger and pried the lids from each of the wooden casks. "What if we cannot reach all four of them, captain? Or if more of the beasts await us on the island?"

"If! If! Do not speak to me of if. What if your aunt had hooves and a camel's hump? There is no use speculating. We must deal with each danger as it arises." Sinbad's voice held slight irritation but he did not look at Byrne. Instead he kept his eyes on the dragons. They were very close now. "Hand me a cask. William, you take one as well, in case I miss."

Byrne obediently did as his master commanded. The carpet swooped and brought them to within a few yards of the leading dragon. Its jaws opened in a snarl. Sinbad ignored it and raised the cask over his head. At the carpet banked hard to the left the creature's jaws snapped shut on empty air and Sinbad hurled the cask at the creature's head. It shattered and splashed liquid all over the thing's scaly face, though it apparently had no effect; Sinbad had at least hoped some might get into the reptile's eyes, but apparently it had not. No matter. He turned and bawled, "Ariadne, another cask! William, you take the one on the right!" Then, to the carpet, "Take us between the other beasts, as close as possible, but keep us out of harm's way!"

The carpet looped and sailed them around the other dragons as commanded. Sinbad and William Byrne took turns heaving the wooden casks at the dragons until all four of the creatures were thoroughly doused. They cawed and snapped at Sinbad and his companions, but the carpet successfully dodged all these attacks.

By now they were almost over the *Blue Nymph* and the longboats. Sinbad commanded the carpet to fly low between the boats and then roared at his men, "It is done! Harpoons to the rail! Bowmen at the ready!"

The reptiles whirled in the air and dived at the boats. As one, Henri Delacrois and his archers dipped their arrowheads in the flaming braziers and then let fly at the dragons. The arrows themselves bounced harmlessly off the scaly hides but that was expected. The important thing was that they served to carry fire to the lamp oil that Sinbad and William Byrne had splashed all over the winged lizards, and all four of the beasts were suddenly engulfed in flame. They screeched in agony, flapping and flailing in midair in a vain effort to extinguish the flames.

Now, as rehearsed, the remaining crew aboard the *Blue Nymph* braced themselves and hurled their harpoons at the dragons, the spears each trailing a line behind them. The beasts, still spinning madly in mid-air as they tried to understand what was happening to them, were unprepared for this new assault and though the missiles could not penetrate the scaly armor any more than the arrows had, nevertheless the lines they carried entangled the reptiles hopelessly. Their panicky thrashing and flapping of their leathery wings actually made it worse; the more the beasts struggled, the more they wrapped the ropes around themselves and each other, and those lines had been carefully treated by Omar and his men to be flameproof. All four beasts, screaming and aflame, now unable to even use their wings to escape, plummeted to the waves.

A cheer arose from the boats. Omar and Delacrois barked orders as the ship swung around, cutting between the beasts. Now the longboats were coming up on them as well, and nets were cast forth. The beasts shrieked in rage and pain, wings flapping and claws pawing madly at the lines, but they were not swimmers. The longboats were on them now and the men of the *Blue Nymph* were hacking at the dying beasts with swords and spears.

"The eyes!" Delacrois was yelling. "Spears through the eyes and into the brain!"

Above, on the carpet, Sinbad nodded as he saw his men descend on the drowning reptiles. "They will make short work of them now."

"I am impressed," Ariadne admitted. "I had not thought it possible to defeat the beasts."

"A man can always out-think a beast." Sinbad grinned, but it was harsh and without humor. "I learned this from your own Ralf. His people hunted the great leviathan whales in the northern latitudes. It was he who first taught my men the techniques of harpoon and net they used. The flaming arrows were Henri's refinement. But the beasts are of little concern compared to the wizards who guide them," he added. "The true challenge still awaits us. We must gain entry to this tower." He directed his words to the carpet now. "Take us to the top of the Obsidian Isle."

The carpet swung smoothly in a loop and turned west, bearing its three riders into the setting sun.

On the *Blue Nymph*, Tishimi Osara stirred and moaned. Her eyes snapped open and she struggled to sit up. Her brow was furrowed with pain and her face slick with sweat. "Captain? Omar?"

No answer. Her vision swam for a moment and then cleared. The cabin was empty. She heard shouts and the patter of running feet out on the deck. She threw off the sleeping silks and swung her legs around, her bare feet hitting the planks. Swaying, she stood, one hand braced on the bunk to steady herself. She saw her leathers and blades lying on the cabin floor and reached for them.

Moments later, clad once more in her battle attire, she staggered out on to the deck. There she saw Omar at the tiller, shouting orders at the men to bring the longboats back on board and stow the gear. "No! Omar, stop! We must not!"

Rafi was suddenly at her side, steadying her. "Easy, Tishimi," he said. "It is good that you are awake but you must rest, your injury was severe."

"Never mind that!" She flung his hand away and strode to where Omar was at the tiller. "Omar, please," she said. "The captain—I must speak to him. We are deceived. There is great danger—"

Omar blinked. "It is good to see you, Tishimi, but—" He gestured towards the west. "Captain Sinbad is already gone. He and Byrne and the woman Ariadne have gone after Ralf."

"No!" Tishimi paled, then steadied. "Then we must follow. I need a longboat—oarsmen—"

"It is useless," Rafi had reached her by then, and laid a hand on her shoulder. "Tishimi, we have no way to ascend to the lair of the Mages. Look." He pointed at the obsidian cliffs in the distance. "It is impossible to climb that," he said. "Hundreds of feet high and made of black glass. Even the captain must employ an enchantment. I do not think we can duplicate it without the girl Ariadne—and she is with Sinbad."

Tishimi's eyes narrowed. She saw the braziers laden with hot coals that the crewmen were unloading from the longboats. "There are other ways," she said. "My people know how to reach such a height without the need of any magic. I need sailcloth and lines. But we must hurry. Omar, we must!" she added as she saw the old seaman about to protest. "The girl leads them into a trap."

"And you want us to follow them into it," Omar growled. He glared at the Asian woman.

She in turn met his gaze with the resolve that Omar knew to be as unshakable as tempered steel. "I will go alone if I must. But I am going."

At last Omar sighed, "Very well. What do you want us to do?"

Tishimi told him.

The enchanted carpet carried Sinbad and his companions above cliffs of black glass. The sun was nearly beyond the horizon now, the skies a deep purple. Behind them, to the east, stars were already visible. Byrne asked, "How long to moonrise?"

"Not long." Sinbad was grim. He unsheathed the scimitar and held it ready. "This is not battle. We stand little chance against wizards or demons. We must move in stealth, free Ralf, and then fly back to the ship. But that means if we encounter any guards, any acolytes, they must be silenced instantly and permanently. You understand this?"

William Byrne nodded. Ariadne paled a little, but after a moment she nodded as well.

Satisfied, Sinbad commanded the carpet, "Land us there, near the crest."

The carpet sailed them to where Sinbad pointed and settled gently on to the surface of the cliff. The three stepped off, their boots crunching softly on the glass pebbles. There was little light left to see by now, but enough for Ariadne to discern a small pathway leading downward into a hollow a few feet from the cliff's edge. As they approached they saw stairs hewn out of the rock, spiraling down into a tunnel.

"One hopes they will not anticipate attack from above," Byrne whispered.

Sinbad nodded. "We are gambling that they assume the dragons are sufficient safeguard," he whispered in reply. "Silently now."

Byrne and Ariadne obediently fell into step behind him. The three tiptoed down the steps into the tunnel, guiding themselves by keeping one hand on the wall. Soon the stairs ended and the path leveled out, and they could see a faint red glow ahead.

They emerged into a circular chamber with a giant slab of obsidian in the center that rose waist-high, like a table. It was the source of the light. There was an unearthly glow flickering within it that was difficult to look upon; though it was not bright, it was nevertheless discomfiting to the eye and Sinbad had to avoid gazing directly at it. Behind this slab, shackled to the wall, hung Ralf Gunarson. He was unconscious.

"Ralf!" Sinbad was at his side in an instant, examining the shackles. "William! Help me with these. We must get him away from this place."

"I think not, Captain Sinbad." This was from a hooded man who had just entered the chamber. Behind him shambled a dozen figures that moved slowly and awkwardly, vaguely human in appearance, but with deep brownish-red leathery skin. With horror Sinbad saw that there were only empty sockets where their eyes should have been. "Take them," the robed man commanded.

The man-things shuffled forward. Sinbad and William Byrne had their blades out and ready, but the creatures batted them away as though they were merely children playing with sticks, and seized the two men with their gnarled, clawlike hands. Then they stopped, waiting for further instruction.

Three more robed figures entered the chamber. Sinbad said, "Very well, you have the advantage. Who are you? What is this about? Where is Balthazar?"

"I am here, captain." The robed man threw back his hood to reveal Balthazar's plump face, no longer wearing a jolly grin, but rather a thin, calculating smile. "We are the Five, the Keepers of the Obsidian Shard."

"I see only four," William Byrne blurted.

"The fifth came with you. My daughter." Balthazar's smile grew slightly wider. "You did well, my dear."

They had forgotten Ariadne. Now she stepped forward to join the other four robed ones. She turned to face the two men of the *Blue Nymph* and Sinbad saw her eyes were wet. "I am sorry, Captain," she said. "But it was the only way." She turned back to her father. "I brought him, as I said. Now you must keep your end of the bargain. Release the northerner to me and we will go."

Aboard the *Blue Nymph*, Omar was shaking his head at Tishimi Osara. "No. It will never work."

"I have seen it done!" Tishimi glared back up at Sinbad's irascible second-in-command. "It is used to carry holiday lanterns, messages—"

"It cannot be done from a longboat," Omar cut in sharply. "Not on that scale. We need the speed of sail and wind; it has to be from the ship. We shall have to bring the *Blue Nymph* in close to the base of the cliffs. At night. In unknown waters. There could be rocks, a reef—and the tides are not with us. We could smash this vessel to kindling. To say nothing of the risk to you."

"I will take the risk. And you know the Captain would risk the ship for any of his crewmen. He has done it. More than once. Can we do less for him?" Tishimi shot back. "I do not ask you to fight, just to help me reach him! I ask you to *sail*! In all the oceans there is no one that knows more of sailing vessels than you, old man, and no ship finer and more maneuverable than this one! You have said so yourself! Did you lie?"

"Very well, you have the advantage. Who are you?"

Omar's brows knitted into a furious scowl. "By Allah, woman, were you a man—"

"Were *you* a man instead of an old maid we would not be arguing!" Tishimi snapped. Then she realized what she had said and fell silent.

For a moment neither one spoke.

Omar said quietly, "You forget yourself. And your oaths."

Tishimi dropped her eyes. "Yes. I am sorry, Omar. I know you are a man of courage and valor. But what else is there? We have no magic for this. We must use our wits and our skill."

"Skill is what is telling me your plan is impossible. The fire cannot be built high enough aboard ship, let alone a longboat, and there is no beach. We need to carry a man, not a party lantern." Omar's eyes slitted. Something, the wisp of an idea, was hovering at the edge of his thoughts, a butterfly of inspiration that, could he but grasp it... "Sail," he breathed. "That is it. You ask me to sail, woman? That is what we shall do. Haroun!" he bellowed. "More lines! All we have left!" He turned back to Tishimi. "And we need another man, a warrior to accompany you."

"I ask no man to accompany me," Tishimi began. "Only—"

"Do you want my knowledge or not?" Omar waved her to silence. "It is a problem of wind and sail and waves, and that is what I know. You said so. Did *you* lie?"

Tishimi could not help smiling. "No, old man, I did not."

"Then believe me when I tell you: it cannot be done with one person, it would tear your arms from your sockets. It must be two."

Tishimi considered it for a moment, then nodded assent. "Very well. Who shall it be?"

"Delacrois, I think. He is thin enough." Omar smiled in return, then turned aft and roared, "Henri! We need you!"

Sinbad stared at Ariadne in disbelief. "This cannot be—Tishimi's soul-sword—we would have known!" he exploded, finally. "How in the name of the devil—"

"The Asian woman's sword would have detected any spell I placed on Ralf, yes." Ariadne shook her head. "But I placed no such spell. There is no deceit. I love him. And you!" she added, whirling to glare at her father. "You were to leave him for me! You were not to harm Ralf at all! Why did you not bid the dragons to just take the captain as we discussed? We had a bargain!"

"Yes, but—" Balthazar shrugged. "I saw the ship. I saw the warriors on board. Not just this one but also his companions—the swordswoman, the archer. I realized that the crystal was not showing us the man but the *vessel*. The *Blue Nymph* is the answer to the question we put to the Shard, when we asked it to show us the latest candidate for the prophecy. No one man aboard is the mightiest warrior but all together, they are the mightiest warriors. Enough to feed the Shard for three generations. And I was right!" he added, his expression fierce. "Gods below, did you not see? They *bested the dragons!* With ropes and sticks and oil!" He spread his hands helplessly. "I dared not risk you fleeing with the Norseman. By taking him, I insured you would bring the entire ship to me."

Balthazar turned back to Sinbad. "It is not so black," he said. "The Shard takes only the soul. You and your crew will still have life of a sort. The men that hold you were once like you, until the Shard took them. They still live, and they serve us. It is a sacrifice worth making to preserve the knowledge we have gained here. We have spent centuries on this island, gazing into the heart of the Shard, learning the secrets of that which forms the substance of the universe. We command forces you cannot even comprehend. Against that, what are the lives of a merchant seaman and his crew of vagabonds and misfits, eh? You should be volunteering to help us! It is for the betterment of mankind!"

"It is a prison!" Sinbad spat. "Not just for the mindless husks that hold us, but for you as well! You dare not leave the isle! You do not plan to let the girl leave, either! You know it is so! Tell her!"

"You lie!" Ariadne stepped forward and slapped Sinbad across the face. "We can leave whenever we wish! Your crew will feed the Shard for years to come! Ralf and I will be together! He already agreed to leave your ship to be with me! You are just trying to turn us against each other!"

Sinbad ignored her. He was watching something else. "Is that so, Balthazar?" he asked, casually, playing for time. "You would risk all your secrets on this lovesick girl?"

"It was a fair bargain. How many lives on your vessel, captain? Twenty? Thirty? At one each seven years, they will sustain us for a century or more." Balthazar dismissed it with a wave. "We can afford to let my daughter have her northern lover."

"For a time," Sinbad said. "But he will age. She will not. Is that not so? Does Ralf's life also measure in centuries now, girl?"

"I would make it so." Ariadne, for the first time, looked uncertain. "It can be done."

"But then he would know you for what you are." Sinbad's voice was low, steady. "He would know that you are a liar and a witch. That you killed his shipmates in some hellish rite to gain this gift for him. Isn't that so?"

"He will never know!" Ariadne's voice was shrill and desperate. "We will be gone! You will be dead! Who will tell him?"

"You just did." Sinbad smiled. "Your lover is awake, witch. Ask him what he thinks of your murder and sorcery."

Ariadne whirled to face the wall behind her and the other mages, where Ralf was still shackled. All had forgotten him save Sinbad, who had seen him stirring and fought to keep everyone talking until the giant was awake enough to comprehend what was happening. Now the Norseman was staring at Ariadne, his face a mask of horror and betrayal. "Ariadne, no. No. No."

Then Sinbad saw something else, something that etched horror on his own face. Through the hazy gray-black glass of the obsidian wall, he could see the beginning of the moonrise over the sea.

They were out of time.

The first glimmer of moonrise that so alarmed Captain Sinbad actually saved the *Blue Nymph* and the lives of all aboard her.

Omar was at the tiller, with Tishimi and Delacrois on either side of him, aft, each frantically knotting lines about themselves. Omar ignored them. He was watching the cliffs and the spray and the sea as the *Blue Nymph* picked up speed, riding the tide toward the obsidian cliff face before them. He bellowed to Haroun in the rigging. "More sail! Faster!"

Then the moonlight shone and Omar suddenly saw a glistening black lump directly in their path. He swore. "Tishimi! Henri! It must be now! Heave! For your lives!" He did not pause to see if he was obeyed but yanked hard on the tiller, and the *Blue Nymph* jinked and spun at such an angle that it seemed all aboard would be flung off into the sea to dash out their brains on the rocks.

At the same time Henri Delacrois and Tishimi Osara flung the lines that bound them into the air and between them billowed a sail of their own, a sail that filled and flew up and out from the stern of the *Blue Nymph*, carrying Tishimi and Henri with it. A single rope unspooled from the deck, hissing like a snake as the sail filled and rose. The *Blue Nymph* tacked hard and spun, facing back out into the sea with her stern to the cliff face, so that now Tishimi and Henri were riding on the improvised parasail directly upward to the top of the cliff.

"Omar!" Haroun was shouting now. "We go too far! There is not enough rope!"

It was the speed of the ship pulling the sail that kept Tishimi and Henri in the sky—but there was no way to turn the ship for another try without the two of them dropping like stones. Omar muttered a profanity that was half curse and half desperate prayer. He scooped up a hatchet from the deck and cut the line, gambling that momentum would be enough to carry the two warriors the rest of the way to the top of the cliff. Even that stolen second with his hands off the tiller almost did them in and he was only just able to catch hold and turn the ship from another rock that was barely visible under the roiling seas. His eyes on the waves, Omar dared not look behind him to see if Tishimi and Henri had made it. "Are they safe?" he roared at Haroun, who was still in the rigging.

"I cannot see—by Allah! Omar, we must flee! Something is happening at the cliff! The glass—it is on fire!"

Omar cursed again and made for open sea.

Ariadne sobbed and flung herself through the gathering to fall against Ralf's massive chest. "Please— my love—"

"No." Ralf's voice was a hoarse rasp. "You must—not. We cannot—you cannot—" Now his eyes were wet as well. "It's *wrong*," he burst out, finally. "You know it's wrong. You cannot ask me to start our lives together with—this."

Balthazar had lost all patience. One-handed, he grasped Ariadne by the shoulder and threw her across the chamber. "Enough!" he snarled. "Let him die with his shipmates then! The Shard must feed! It is moonrise!"

"No!" Ariadne shrieked. "You shall not have him! Not after all I—"

Balthazar's hand sketched red fire in the air. Ariadne's hands lifted instantly in response and blue fire arced forth to meet Balthazar's. There was the crackle and snap of energy—*lightning*, Sinbad thought. *Sorcerer's weapons. This battle will fry us like spitted fish and they'll not even notice.*

Then Tishimi Osara and Henri Delacrois burst into the room, and all hell really did break loose. Delacrois was hacking vainly at the red shamblers with his short sword, but Tishimi had better luck with her katana; proof against all magics, Sinbad remembered. Of course. In seconds four of the red things lay headless on the floor. The other robed mages flinched before her blade. Both raised their hands before them in defense, the palms just beginning to flicker with eldritch fire and Tishimi let out a laugh that was almost a snarl. Her katana flashed in a double arc and the wizards screamed in horror as their severed hands fell to the floor. "Weave your glamours with bleeding stumps, then, hellspawn," she spat. "Captain! Hold fast!"

Sinbad and Byrne had taken advantage of the distraction to struggle free. They reclaimed their weapons and slashed at the mindless red men. Tishimi and Henri fought to join them and in seconds they were shoulder to shoulder. "Flying wedge," Sinbad said. "Tishimi in the lead. Get us to Ralf." The red men were going down and when it was Tishimi's blade cutting at them, they stayed down; but more were pouring in to the room from the entrance, blocking them from where Ralf hung chained to the wall.

Ariadne and Balthazar were still locked in their duel. Sparks flew as their hands flickered and wove increasingly rapid patterns in the air. They seemed evenly matched but there was a building hum of energies between them that, Sinbad was sure, would soon reach a crescendo that none of them would live through. He shouted, "Ariadne! Help us! Let us save your love at least!"

Ariadne's gaze locked briefly with his. She nodded, then glanced at the slab in the center of the chamber. "Sister!" she called out to Tishimi. "It is your warrior's arm that can save us all!"

It took Sinbad a second to comprehend it, but Tishimi was already in motion. She swung the katana in a mighty arc that cleared a path, not to Ralf, but to the obsidian slab in the center of the room.

Suddenly Balthazar paled in realization of what was coming. He screamed, "*No! Not the Shard! Fool of a daughter! What have you done?*"

Tishimi Osara lifted the soulsword as high as she could and brought it chopping down on the glass slab with all the strength she had.

The slab did not shatter so much as explode in a cascading shower of red energy and glittering dust. As it went, there was a sound that later Sinbad would say was not quite a scream, not quite the peal of a bell, not quite breaking glass, but it had all these qualities; and Delacrois would only ever say that sometimes yet he heard it in nightmares. There was a great whoosh as all the souls held trapped in the fragment spun free to flee to whatever otherworldly dimension waited for them. The Obsidian

Shard gave up its illusion of life in that unholy shriek, and so did all that it supported. The red things collapsed where they stood, fallen marionettes with their strings cut. Balthazar fell as well, and Sinbad saw his skin shrivel and peel away from bones that were themselves already rotting to dust.

Ariadne collapsed along with him. Ralf lunged, the shackles still holding him, and then they snapped free. He fell to her side. "My love— no—you cannot—"

Ariadne's face smiled up at him; it was not the face they had known. Her hair was white and falling out, her skin as seamed and brown as a walnut. It continued to age and crack as they all stared in wonder. She turned her gaunt hag's face to Ralf and smiled, shakily. "See me as I truly am," she whispered. "I am so sorry. I am dying, but— Do you love me still, a little, my Norseman?"

"Always." Ralf could barely choke the word out.

"Then I die happy." She struggled to sit up and Ralf lifted her into his arms. "No, no, too late for me," she said. "This whole island was caught up in the spell of the Shard; it should have sunk beneath the waves centuries gone. Now finally it will die too. But you still have a chance. Captain Sinbad, the carpet will still fly for you while I yet live. You must take it and escape with your crew before I am gone too. Now! You have only moments! See, the walls are already cracking!"

It was true. They fled back through the passage up the steps to the top of the cliff. Blessedly, the enchanted carpet was where they had left it. Ralf refused to leave Ariadne's body, even though it was hardly more than a gnarled mummy in rags by that point. Yet it still moved.

Ralf clutched the skeletal figure desperately to him. "Captain, hurry— Rafi might know of some—" His voice trailed off. The others turned away, unable to bear the agony on the Viking's coarse features.

Sinbad said, "Get us clear of this. Take us to the *Blue Nymph*."

The carpet lifted them up and out, and in seconds they had the *Blue Nymph* in sight. Sinbad thought they might actually make it as they swooped in close—but then the enchanted carpet crumpled beneath them and it was just a bit of tapestry again. They all tumbled into the water.

Sinbad broke the surface and saw Tishimi, Ralf, William, and Henri bob up each in turn as well. "Swim for it!" he told them, then bellowed, "Ahoy the *Blue Nymph*! Lower a boat!"

Omar and Haroun were already doing so, he saw. For a moment he thought Ralf was going to dive to look for Ariadne's body, but then he saw Ralf himself realize how fruitless that would be. Instead, the Norseman simply floated, not moving.

Behind them, there was a great shuddering and rumbling as the Obsidian Isle sank beneath the waves. Sinbad watched it go, and thought, irrationally, that the sea itself seemed relieved to be rid of it. He turned and swam for the longboat Omar was bringing to them. He could see that Tishimi and Henri were already on it, and Haroun was dragging Byrne aboard as well.

Ralf Gunarson said nothing, but simply struck out for the ship, ignoring the longboat. None dared say anything to dissuade him.

Two days later, Tishimi Osara found Ralf on the aft deck, staring moodily out to sea. "We land in Aghrapur tomorrow," she said.

The Norseman merely grunted.

"Are you leaving the ship then?"

At that, Ralf turned to face her, glowering. "Are you making sport of me?" His voice was rough and Tishimi realized with a start that the big man was on the verge of weeping.

"No. I grieve with you." Tishimi paused, unsure of what to say. After a moment, she added softly, "Ralf, you must know that she loved you."

"She deceived me. She was going to murder us all." His voice cracked a little. "It was a lie and I believed it. Because I am a fool."

"It was not a lie." Tishimi's voice sharpened. "Hear me now, or you *are* a fool. The katana my father gave me revealed nothing save her true face when I happened to glimpse its reflection. There was no spell, no enchantment, no magic of any kind about what passed between you; none save that which you kindled in her heart." Hesitantly, awkwardly, she put a hand on his shoulder. "Love makes fools of us all. She sought only to escape the trap of that cursed island with you, and when she found she could not, she sacrificed all so we could live. She gave up *eternity*. For you. No one—*no* one—has ever been so loved. Certainly not I, or anyone else on this vessel." She let her hand fall away and drew herself up. "If you must brood, brood on that."

Above, on the foredeck over the captain's cabin, Sinbad and Omar watched as Tishimi walked away, leaving Ralf once again staring out to sea.

"Should we say something to him?" Omar asked.

Sinbad shook his head. "Let them sort it out themselves," he said. "I think Henri might have some sort of party planned ashore. He seems to think a night with some tavern girls will put all aright with our Norseman. 'Get back on the horse once thrown,' he says." His teeth bared in a grin. "I doubt Ralf will take kindly to that suggestion, but the ensuing brawl when Henri proposes it will let the boy work off some anger."

"Your scheming would shame even the merchants of Baghdad." Omar let out a short laugh. "A light hand on the tiller, indeed. And you smile over this! I say again, I am cursed with a shipload of children."

Sinbad's grin got wider. "Yes," he said. "You are. But they are *our* children."

THE END

Sinbad By Way of the Spinner-Rack Seventies

This is another one of those Airship 27 jobs I've been training for since I was about thirteen, when I saw *The Golden Voyage of Sinbad* on a double bill with Ralph Bakshi's *Wizards*. That afternoon at the Lake Theater, along with finding Marvel's *Savage Sword of Conan* on the magazine rack down at the grocery store, were my gateway drugs to sword-and-sorcery pulp fiction. Not just the classics like Robert E. Howard and Fritz Leiber, but also things like John Jakes' *Brak the Barbarian,* Lin Carter's *Thongor of Lost Lemuria*, the *Flashing Swords!* anthologies— the paperback racks were just swimming in the stuff throughout my high school years and I was pretty much in for all of it, even down to stuff like *IronJaw* or *Balzan of the Cat People.* If it had a Frazetta cover—or even a Boris Vallejo or a Jeff Jones one—I was all over that action. I'm a little more discriminating these days, but I'm still a fan.

It was an ongoing frustration, though, how badly movies missed the mark most of the time. You'd get stuff that was *almost* good like *The Sword and the Sorcerer,* but nothing ever quite matched up to the delight of that first *Golden Voyage.* Not even *Sinbad and the Eye of the Tiger,* though I do like that one quite a bit. (For that matter, you can make a pretty good case that Ray Harryhausen's three Sinbad movies are about three different guys; they don't really have anything in common.)

So when I got the assignment for a Sinbad story, I just arbitrarily decided that I was doing the *Golden Voyage* version—or as I think of it, the 'real' one. (Those of you that insist that *Seventh Voyage* or *Eye of the Tiger* or some other version is the real one, I'm not going to litigate it with you. You go to your church and I'll go to mine and we'll leave it at that.)

Therefore, at least in my head, this is *that* Sinbad. Those that know the movie will spot confirmation of this here and there, though I tried not to make it oppressive. My feeling is that the new additions to the Sinbad mythology from Airship 27, Ralf and Tishimi and Omar and all the rest, are on that ship as well, we just didn't see them in the movie. I grew quite fond of them as I wrote this, though, and as I was working out the crew dynamics and character interactions I found myself thinking just as much about John Ford's *Stagecoach* and the TV show *Firefly* as I was anything to do with Ray Harryhausen's movies. I tried to put across the idea that this is a family more than a crew, and to make sure everyone had something to do.

As far as the story itself, well, this is basically the Robert E. Howard movie I always wished Ray Harryhausen had made; a kind of bounce off Howard's Conan story *The People of the Black Circle.* My favorite part of that story was always how the evil wizard Khemsa was tempted away from the Black Seers of Yimsha by the hot slave girl who says to him, more or less, *Why are you up in that tower meditating with those weird old wizards all the time when you could be using your magic to hang out with me and get rich? We could rule the world and live large and have a lot of sex!* It doesn't work out for Khemsa; the Seers take a terrible vengeance on him and the whole thing is kind of a side plot from Conan having to rescue the Devi Yasmina from the Black Seers anyway. Nevertheless, the idea of the immortal wizard getting tempted by earthbound romance always struck me as a really powerful idea. Plus, I wanted to do something to involve the crew as opposed to just something important to Sinbad himself, and this story sort of wove itself out of that.

I did research—I always do. You don't need that much for a story where magic works and you are making up whole cities and cursed obsidian islands and so on out of whole cloth, but I do want to point out that in the earliest translations of the *Arabian Nights* the first flying carpet really was allegedly ridden by one Prince Husain of the Indies. Also you should know that kites, parasails, and hot-air balloons date back to the second century A.D. in Asia, and were used for military purposes even then; so it's not unreasonable that Tishimi and Omar would be aware of the technology, as well-traveled as they are. I read up a little on sailing as well, although the Harryhausen Sinbad sails on a ship that's not exactly period-accurate. I was more worried about staying consistent with the ship we saw in the movies rather than realistically depicting the frankly unpleasant and unhygienic sailing experience Sinbad's peers actually endured on the high seas in the eighth century. No need to derail the fun train.

Anyway, it's not so much about accuracy as it is about *tone.* The Harryhausen Sinbad we are trying to evoke in these books was a wonderful hot mess of about equal parts Greek mythology, Arabian Nights, and Hollywood swashbuckler, and that's what I tried to give this. A special shout-out goes to the amazing Brian Clemens, the co-writer of *Golden Voyage* with Ray Harryhausen and also the creator of about half of everything I ever loved out of British TV, including Emma Peel, *The Persuaders,* and Harry Rule. Clemens also gave us *Captain Kronos*

Vampire Hunter, another DVD that's usually in pretty heavy rotation around here. He's no longer with us, sadly, but I felt his shadow very much over this story, particularly his ear for dialogue. This one is absolutely for his memory, and if you don't know his work, you definitely should check it out.

Thanks as always to the beta reading crew: Anne Hawley, Lorinda Adams, Brekke Ferguson, Tiffany Tomcal, Sena Friesen, and Ed Bosnar. And of course to my wife Julie, who let me run all three of the Harryhausen *Sinbad* DVDs three or four times over the last month and call it research. I am so spoiled.

And thanks to *you*, Constant Reader, for checking out our stuff in the first place. I hope you all enjoyed this and that I get a chance to do it again.

GREG HATCHER - is a writer and schoolteacher from Burien, Washington. He has been published in various places since 1992 and is a three-time winner of the Higher Goals Award for Children's Writing. For eleven years he wrote a weekly column on comics for Comic Book Resources.com, and today he does much the same sort of weekly column on popular culture in general at Atomic Junk Shop.com. Pulp and adventure fiction remains his first love, though, and writing stories for Airship 27's various anthologies is one of his favorite gigs. In addition to writing, he also teaches the Cartooning and Young Authors classes as part of an after-school arts program for grades 7 through 12. He lives in an apartment just south of downtown with his wife Julie, their cat Maggie, and ten thousand books and comics.

Made in the USA
Lexington, KY
15 December 2019

58603403R00092